The Sabbath Garden

The Sabbath Garden

PATRICIA BAIRD GREENE

LODESTAR BOOKS
Dutton   New York

Library of Congress Cataloging-in-Publication Data

Greene, Patricia Baird.
    The Sabbath garden / Patricia Baird Greene—1st ed.
        p. cm.
    Summary: When her elderly Jewish neighbor Solomon Leshko catches her spray-painting her tenement hallway as an expression of her anger and frustration, fourteen-year-old Opie Tyler begins an unusual friendship with him.
    ISBN 0-525-67430-6
    [1. New York (N.Y.)—Fiction. 2. Jews—United States—Fiction. 3. Afro-Americans—Fiction.] I. Title.
PZ7.G8425Sab 1993
[Fic]—dc20   93-19561
                                                                           CIP
                                                                            AC

Published in the United States by Lodestar Books,
an affiliate of Dutton Children's Books,
a division of Penguin Books USA Inc.,
375 Hudson Street, New York, New York 10014

Published simultaneously in Canada
by McClelland & Stewart, Toronto

Editor: Virginia Buckley   Designer: Marilyn Granald
Printed in the U.S.A.   First Edition   10 9 8 7 6 5 4 3 2

This book is dedicated to the people of the Lower East Side, whose courage, humor, and dignity taught me so much during the ten years I lived and worked there; and particularly to the late Liz Christie and all the other Green Guerrillas who started the Bowery-Houston Garden. The garden still flourishes. Go see it if you are ever in New York City.

CONTENTS

ONE

✤

An Outbreak
of Silence

THE SILENCE WAS SO BIG it swallowed the honk and roar of traffic on Second Avenue, swallowed whole blocks of brick tenements and the yellow haze that served as sky over New York City that afternoon.

Opal Tyler tried not to hear the silence as she floated down the sidewalk past familiar stores and street corners that suddenly looked far away. At first, it seemed to come from her friend Conchita Perez. As they walked, Opie stole hungry sideways glances at Conk, who looked perfect and painted—green eye shadow, red fingernails, black hair flying over her shoulders. But Conk walked along, untouched and untouchable, as if she didn't care about the silence.

The girl usually chattered the whole ten blocks home from school—about boys who had tried (successfully) to kiss her, about clothes she would buy down on Delancey Street. Conk was beautiful when she talked—eyes rolling and sparkling, hands tumbling around, full wide mouth laughing, then pursed in a pout. There was a life in Conk that made things seem better. Even when Opie didn't listen to all the words, the lilting sound surrounded her, calmed that tight place down inside.

On their side of the street deep purple shadows had crept across the sidewalk, cooling the simmer of the day. Store owners rolled in their squeaky awnings. Men in undershirts played dominoes on the stoops and old women leaned dreaming out of windows. Opie loved the Second Avenue sidewalk, where no one noticed what a strange pair they were—she and Conk. No one razzed Conchita, who had won a beautiful baby contest at two, for being Puerto Rican and walking with a skinny, gap-tooth black girl. For a little while Opie could forget the stares and rude comments of the Puerto Rican girls at school, the ones who were sucking Conk into their tight little gang.

She hated the reflection of her brown face moving across the luncheonette window. There was the same ugly girl in the next window and the next—hunched over like something heavy had climbed up on her back. She sighed and straightened up her shoulders, but that just made her look bony under the loose white T-shirt.

It exasperated everyone—always telling her to stand up straight! But the only time she would stand all the way up was on the basketball court, where she was a star. Then she didn't care if other people saw her, because when she leaped like a dancer and blocked that ball, their eyes said she was good, and being good broke open the tight feeling in her chest.

But most times she curled over, like now, hoping everyone would excuse her for being so tall and ugly and flat-chested. Tossing her newly straightened hair, she looked away in utter disgust. Stupid hair—combed Brillo dipped in grease—not at all like Conk's hair gloriously streaming over her shoulders. She looked over at the girl, who still hadn't said a word. Conk walked with head thrown back and lips parted, as if she couldn't drink in enough of this hot, heavy June afternoon and had somewhere super important to go anyway.

Suddenly Conk stopped flat in the middle of the sidewalk, hands on her hips, and turned. Opie swerved to avoid bumping into her and thought, Uh oh, here it comes, whatever it is.

"*Caray!* Stop *bugging* me!" Conk yelled, eyes flashing like black diamonds.

2

"Have I said one word?" Opie asked innocently.

"Think I didn't see you watching me? Why don't you get lost!" Conk turned on her heel and stomped off, her bottom pushing up and down beneath her miniskirt in a way that made men turn and make little clucking noises. Opie's stomach knotted up. This was serious. Before she might have shrugged and told herself, Aw, Conk's just overheated again. Sometimes the girl woke up mad and kept jabbing at Opie all day, but she always came around wanting to make up. Then she'd cry real hard while Opie hugged her tight.

Not knowing what else to do, Opie followed, her mind desperately picking through their day for some sign of trouble. Kids celebrated on the last day of school—right? Started out that way. The eighth-grade crowd had burst out of Junior High 25 like a rocket, parading down Eleventh Street with radios blaring, dancing on trash cans, swinging on fire escapes, ripped-up test papers flying in the air like confetti. They were out, permanently out, graduated out! But after Opie and Conk split off and headed south toward their building, the silence had crept up and—blam!—sat right down between them.

Opie was halfway across Fourth Street before she realized that Conk had disappeared. Wheeling around, she walked reluctantly back to the corner, where the crazy girl was smoothing her skirt and peering expectantly into the open door of the Aguadilla Bar and Grill with its green neon palm tree in the window.

Opie hated Fourth Street. Too many things changed hands on the corner of Fourth and Second Avenue. Boys leaned on the graffiti-covered wall by the Aguadilla under the sign that said NO LOITERING in big block letters. They laughed and sassed everyone like they owned the street, sitting on the row of smashed-up metal trash cans, smoking all kinds of things, drinking out of bottles in paper bags.

Conk nervously passed her jean jacket from one arm to the

other, then struck a stance, hand on hip, jacket hanging over it. The boys on the trash cans fell silent midlaugh, elbowed each other, and stared.

At that moment, Opie's older brother, Frank, appeared in the door of the bar. Her brother was the best-looking dude who hung out on Fourth Street. His hair was wavy black and long, his cheekbones high and perfect, and he had strange sexy gold eyes always sliding here and there under half-closed lids. He was a pretty olive color, too, all of which he had lucked into from his half–Puerto Rican father. When he wasn't wound up tight enough to bust, he walked this loose rippling walk, almost like a dance, that made girls stop and stare after him.

Frank readjusted his backward baseball cap, then pulled his sunglasses halfway down on his nose to give Conk a once-over with his sleepy golden eyes.

"Mmm-mm. Looking fly today, little girl," he said, a self-satisfied grin spreading across his face.

Opie watched his lips move. Her heart was beating so fast it felt like she had just finished a basketball game. *This ain't real*, she told herself. *They gotta be goofing on me.* She looked closely at her brother, ready for him to explode in wild laughter and give her the elbow to let her in on the joke. Instead he acted as if she had interrupted something private and needed to beat it—quick! Pulling Conk's jacket off her arm, he threw it at Opie. It lay there on the sidewalk between them.

Conk lowered her eyes and kicked nervously at a blackened piece of gum on the sidewalk. As she bent to pick up her jacket, the pale curved tops of her breasts oozed over her red tank top.

"You don't mind, do ya, Opie?" she asked in a little-girl whisper, holding out the jacket and seeming almost scared.

Frank wrapped an arm around Conk's shoulders and began steering her away. The boys on the garbage cans hooted. Conk stopped to face Opie.

4

"Listen, tell my mama I'm in church, okay? Confirmation class."

"No way she gonna believe *that* one," Opie said flatly and her voice trembled. Conk had to go right home most afternoons to watch her three-year-old sister, Emilia.

Conk smiled through gritted teeth. "Hey, I'm depending on you," she said, putting an arm around Frank's waist, pressing her body against him in a way that made her breasts ooze again.

"Yeah, be a saint, huh, Oops," Frank said. He gave her shoulder a punch that almost knocked her over and leaned toward her with an evil grin.

"You poking out your lip again, girl."

Opie closed her mouth tight as the two of them jaywalked the wide avenue. Conk immediately started chattering brightly, laughing her wild laugh that always sounded like breaking glass. She flashed adoring eyes up at Frank and raised her mouth to his kiss right there between the swerving, honking lanes of traffic.

Opie turned away as the wave that had been towering over her crashed. It left her washed up on some strange shore where she'd never been before.

One of the boys behind her snickered.

"Looks like you been stood up good, sister!"

Then they were all laughing, making ugly clucking sounds.

"Oh, Frankie boy, you make me *so* hot!"

"Ooo-weee. Sock it to me 'fore I melt."

The sound of their voices made holes in Opie's back. Her new white high tops flew over the gray concrete like angels' wings, over the cracks and gum and litter and spit—faster and faster, jumping the foot-deep pothole on Third Street, dodging the jumble of empty boxes at Malkowski's Fruit Stand. Finally the buzzing voices behind her faded into the roar of traffic.

She stopped, out of breath. Why didn't I warn her? she

thought. Could've said, "Yeah, yeah, he looks fine up on Fourth Street, but get him home, that boy ain't good for nothing. He so mean sometimes he'd cut you up with a dull knife." But Conk would've walked away with him anyway. That was the hurt of it. A rush of white-hot anger shoved its way up and spilled over.

"You don't mind, do ya, Opie?" she said out loud, mimicking Conk's high little-girl voice. "Whatd'ya mean, 'You don't mind'? 'Course I *mind!*" She was bellowing now in her own deep voice, but she didn't care. "You bet your big butt I *mind!*" she yelled after them, fighting back the tears. But only the bag lady passing by turned to look.

Out of the corner of her eye she saw what she always tried not to see—that pale rusty bloodstain on the sidewalk in front of the *bodega* on the corner of Second Street. Its fingers reached down toward the gutter. Usually she and Conk talked extra fast and looked across the street when they passed that corner. The rain never washed that stain away and let them be safe again.

A sudden wave of nausea ran through her. She felt weak, drained, felt like crumpling down into the flooding silence on the dirty pavement—like Jimmy Soto with a ten-inch knife in his gut.

Second Street slid by like a dream—the fenced U-Haul lot with trailers and barking Dobermans on chains; run-down brownstones on the north; her building standing up all alone on the south—a square brick island in a sea of parking lots.

Old man Banjo sat on the building's front stoop, eyes closed, face turned toward the yellow sky. Close beside him was an empty bottle of wine with an unlit cigarette lying across the top. Opie collapsed on the step below him, her mind as blank as the haze that started six stories up where pigeons peeked over the peeling green cornice of their building. A heavy, burned-toast smell had settled on the city—the kind that usually came only in August.

The angry hurt twisted her stomach. How long had Conk and Frank been sneaking around behind her back, laughing at her? Seemed like everyone was doing their thing lately and leaving her right out of it. You a rock, Opal, they said, smiling over their shoulders. Even her mother. Then off they went, leaving her heart lying in pieces. Screw being good, she thought, and kicked the stoop so hard a big piece of patched concrete fell off.

"Life is a rotten trouble. So don't take it out on the building!" boomed a loud voice from above.

Opie shot a quick glance up to the second floor, where Solomon Leshko was leaning out his window, snooping again. Old man spied on everyone. Acted like the landlord's personal policeman. He kept saying what a nice building this had been, a *Jewish* building, he always added with pride. Yeah, before us, Opie thought, before the *shvartzers* and *spics* she'd heard him talking about down at the luncheonette. Now the storefronts of the building were boarded up and scrawled with names (and worse) three layers deep. The front door had been kicked in so many times that the plywood nailed on top of it was splintered. And Solomon Leshko, who was ancient enough to need a cane, was the only Jew left.

"Sorry," she said, to get him off her case, and shoved the fallen piece of cement back into the crack.

But the top of her head prickled. Crazy old man was still staring. She looked up again. There he was, poking through pots of red petunias in his window box, his white beard spreading over his fat belly like Santa Claus. A cat paced back and forth on the windowsill, wiping its tail across his face. Rosie, who was leaning out the first-floor window and who knew everything about everyone, said that Solomon had at least twelve cats in that little apartment.

7

A romantic scene from Rosie's favorite soap opera drifted out of her window. Dominic up on the fourth floor was yelling at his wife again in Italian. Reggae music pulsed in Claude the super's apartment. Her ears carefully collected all the little noises. Any noise brought salvation after the unbearable silence.

From across the street, the lonely *bup-bup* of a basketball echoed.

"Hey, Oops, shoot a few!" called her friend Leroy Patterson through the fence of the basketball court in the vacant lot. Opie was the undisputed champ of the Second Street court— never known to miss a shot. Today she thought seriously for the first time in her life of not playing, but changed her mind and walked slowly across the street, kicking a broken bottle into the gutter.

Leroy was dribbling toward the basket as the gate clanged shut behind her. He dumped a hook shot easily in the hoop and smiled at her. Tall, that boy, over six feet at fifteen, already a superstar on the high school basketball team. She didn't smile back. Leroy had looked funny at her the last few times they played ball—some kinda hunger. Feel like I never wanna see the jerk again, she thought, only Leroy my best basketball partner.

He walked up.

"You gonna stand there a year or two more or you gonna play?" he asked, his face shiny with sweat.

Opie shrugged, leaning back against the fence. Leroy frowned and stared, his eyes looking her all over. Made her want to disappear.

"Oops, you sick or something?"

"You my mother, Leroy?" The hurt was hardening into mean—and she'd been feeling mean toward Leroy and everyone else for a few weeks now. The mood lay like lead on her chest. It didn't let her breathe. "Forget it," she said. "You look pretty dumb hugging that ball."

He shoved the ball at her and backed up, dancing around for her pass. She dribbled madly, swooping in to twist and lay up the ball. Rebound, dribble, spin around the rim, in. Her muscles fell into the familiar movements, comforting her, setting her free. The burden that sat so heavy on her shoulders glided off while she flew over the asphalt.

Leroy moved uncertainly toward her, but she dribbled away, faking him out as he turned to receive the ball. Something hard and sharp filled her and drove her to shoot and shoot again.

Finally, she passed the ball and let him in. He took a wild, off-balance shot from way down the court and missed. She watched the ball bounce out of bounds, then kicked it hard against the wall, walked through the gate, crossed the street, and sat back down on the stoop. Her breath came in noisy gulps. The sweat rolled down the side of her face and her heart pounded in the top of her head. God, what weirdness was taking over her life? she wondered. An hour ago, it was just a dull, ordinary, barely tolerable day, like always. Now it seemed messy and out of shape, dangerous almost.

She shuddered and sat up straight as a streak of orange spray paint shot like a rocket across her mind. She had been thinking all year about spray painting something on a wall somewhere—she had even been drawing pictures in her school notebook.

She looked over again at Banjo, sockless ankle swinging in time to a tune. His gnarled hand with the long, curling fingernails fidgeted back and forth like he was playing a banjo sitting there across his knee. Told her once he had learned banjo from his daddy way back in South Carolina before he came to the city.

Suddenly he looked over at her looking at him and wrapped his long legs around each other like a pretzel, which Opie thought he did because he was ashamed of his pants smelling like pee. Banjo spent his days panhandling for cheap wine.

But he had adopted their building's stoop as his main rest stop and they all knew him. She watched as he settled into his dreams again. Hardware stores in New York City were not stupid enough to sell spray paint to fourteen-year-olds, she thought, but ain't no law 'bout selling it to winos.

She leaned her head back. Solomon Leshko was gone from his window and Rosie was talking on the phone. Something said, *Do it now!* Do something crazy and beyond that maybe break this silence wide open.

Opie bounded up five flights of stairs, three at a time. As she opened the door, she heard the *shush* of the shower, which meant her mother was busy getting ready to go to work cleaning offices uptown. In the bedroom she shared with her mother, she rooted around in the back of her underwear drawer for the plastic L'eggs egg with her baby-sitting money and dumped the crumpled bills on the bed. After grabbing ten dollars for two cans of spray paint, she stuffed an extra dollar in her pocket to get old man Banjo off the stoop and moving on up the Bowery to the hardware store at Cooper Square.

Poking her head into the steamy bathroom, she called out, "Hi, Ma'am." She always called her mother Ma'am. Her grandmother, Queen Bess, had said it was her mother's due. Need some respect at home, Grandma'am had said, if you can't get it nowhere else.

"Hey, sugar," came a tired voice from the shower. "You seen Frank?"

Opie bit her lip. "Oh, he just hanging 'round up on Fourth Street."

"Listen, hon. There's hot dogs and beans, okay?"

Not again, Opie thought. "Yeah. See ya."

Opie flew down the worn marble stairs and smiled at the bottom when she heard Rosie's voice still droning on the phone. Banjo was so eager to buy that paint for her and get his hands on that dollar, he nearly tripped over himself on the steps.

"Take it easy, man!" she called after him. "Orange, remember. Orange and black."

Now Opie trusted the old man, but the Rainbow Bar and Grill lay between Second Street and the hardware store, so as soon as he rounded the corner onto the Bowery, she headed after him to keep an eye on his progress.

At the corner she could see Banjo was weaving a true path up to the hardware store on Cooper Square. Good old Banjo. Then back he came, holding out the bag, wanting to know if there was anything else he could get her. Old man didn't much like panhandling.

TWO

❧

Dark Alley
Never Ending

FRANK NEVER SHOWED FOR DINNER. Slouching at the table in the small yellow kitchen, Opie picked at the gooey canned beans with her fork. The fluorescent light flickered, making her feel unreal and nerved up, but it was too much effort to pull over a chair and give it a whack to make it stop.

Soft early-evening noises and smells of the air shaft drifted in through the kitchen window—sausage sizzling, dishes clinking, voices murmuring, laughing, yelling. For a few minutes the U-shaped air shaft filled with golden light as the sun set; then a line of soft blue shadow crept up the wall.

Opie gave up on eating, pushed her plate away, and lay her head down on her arms. The ache in her chest felt like someone had whammed her with a sledgehammer. That hammer been coming at her for some time now. Been running in front of it in her dreams, scrambling to get out of the way and let it pass on by, even if that meant dying. The dying part was easy—all it took was a bottle of aspirin. But at the hospital they brought her back and set her up, sent her off to see Dr. Jamison, the psychiatrist, who said she didn't have to run scared. But he forgot to take the hammer away.

Didn't see Dr. Jamison no more. Man had certified her cured of wanting to die two months ago and wrote a dismissal to Social Services on a piece of white paper that lay on his clean white blotter that sat on his big white-and-chrome desk in his white office in the hospital. Then he had folded his hands. Folded his hands a lot, Dr. Jamison, maybe to let her know how calm he was, how it was really okay to let it all hang out with him. Opie decided not to scare him with raging and crying. Decided instead to be super good and get out fast so she wouldn't have to squeak around in his puffy white chair with the cold chrome handles every week.

"I like you, Opal," he said at their last visit. She had looked him straight in the eye and smiled sweetly, thinking, White man, you don't know diddly-squat. Under this Sunday dress I got bruises 'round my neck like a string of pearls. Guess who put them there. Me. Your success story. Ain't gonna kill myself in big doses no more, 'cause everyone gets too upset. Just gonna die kinda silent. And by the way, big man, she thought as he showed her out of the office, you should see my mother these days after you gave her those little yellow pills to calm her down. She got onto those pills in a big way and now they make her sleep all day. It's a ton of fun 'round my house.

A door slammed upstairs in Conk's apartment. Opie chewed feverishly on her only remaining fingernail and held her breath. Marita Perez's voice took off in scolding Spanish. Conk was home. The yelling and screaming went roller-coastering overhead for twenty minutes, rising to an unbearable pitch.

From a window across the air shaft someone yelled, *"Shut up!"* There was a five-second silence, then another scream as plates crashed and pots banged against the wall. Opie stood up and dialed Conk to remind her to come down and get her jacket. They had a pact to save each other from their mothers that way.

As she paced the narrow apartment hallway waiting for

13

Conk's knock, she wanted to punch a hole in the wall. Wished she could think of something to say mean enough to make the girl cry, but her mind was blank again. Anyway, Conk hadn't really banged that hammer into her; she had felt it coming ever since Grandma'am died. Maybe this silence was better than the dread.

Conk stood in her rumpled red top with black smudges of eye makeup on her cheeks, her perfect hair limp and tangled. She sighed a big, trembly sigh as she pushed past Opie into the bedroom that Opie shared with Ma'am.

"*Ay,* is it crazy up there!" she said, waving her hand toward the ceiling. She plopped on Opie's pink-quilted bed, kicking off her red boots. Suddenly she burst out laughing.

"My mother is such an ass. She broke three plates—and you know, she missed me." Conk rolled her eyes. "She better save a few for what's coming." She seemed back to her old self.

Opie stood nervously turning the bedroom door handle behind her, wondering what *was* coming but not really wanting to find out. "She don' know 'bout Frank, does she?" she asked Conk, surprised at how flat her voice sounded. The idea of Conk and Frank had burned down to a sour ache in the bottom of her stomach.

"All she knows is there wasn't any confirmation class this afternoon. But I said, 'Mama, I *was* in church. I said a special rosary for Uncle Jorge.' He died last week. Oh well. She didn't believe me."

Conk shrugged, bounced off the bed, and bent down in front of the mirror over the vanity to wipe off the smeared eye makeup.

"Ain't told no one 'bout Frank—don't you neither, you hear?" Conk looked up sharply at Opie in the mirror with her don't-give-me-any-flak look.

"You *hear?*" she asked again loudly. Opie usually gave

Conk no flak, even if she felt like it, which was often. It was part of the price she paid for the skinny little pieces of friendship that Conk doled out.

"Got any Kleenex?" Conk asked.

Opie brought the Kleenex box from the bathroom and threw it on the vanity. She watched Conk open her mother's cold cream jar and rub two greasy pink blobs into her cheeks.

"How long you two been sneaking 'round?" Opie asked.

"Longer than you think." Conk smiled triumphantly at herself in the mirror as she combed and fluffed up her hair.

Opie closed her eyes and leaned against the wall for support. The fragile world of shared everything she had worked so hard to coax out of Conk all these years was shattered into a million pieces in one afternoon. Her mind sifted through the rubble. She knew they hadn't been *real* friends, like when you wanted to be with each other every minute and neither was ranking on the other, since the beginning of sixth grade, when Conk decided boys were the most important thing in life.

"Shoulda known I can't trust you no more with all these boys," Opie said, sitting down on her mother's bed with her hands in her lap.

Conk wheeled around. "Come on, Oops. Have I ever lied to you 'bout liking your brother? *Have I?*"

Opie stared straight through her. It was true that Conk had been sighing around about Frank since she was ten. Indris Brown, who had a new baby she was telling everyone was Frank's, had said to Conk that Frank reminded her of an Inca god in the history book. Frank thought he was some kind of god, too—accepted everyone's offerings without thanks and when they were rude enough not to offer, he took anyway.

"Now I just *got* him, that's all!" Conk said, laughing her wild laugh and falling back on the bed. "Mmm-mm, he is so beautiful! I love him." Throwing her arms around herself, she

15

curled her toes and looked toward the ceiling in a flurry of dreams.

The lump in Opie's throat was so big, the words could hardly come out. Suddenly she got it. It was *her* fault—this mess. How could Conk know what Frank was really like now? All these years Opie had been making herself seem big by laying a heavy hero rap on her brother, who was busy turning evil.

"That boy got mean secrets you don't wanna know," Opie warned. "How you gonna handle his ugly stuff when he starts laying it on you?" She left off saying, Maybe wake up some morning and he's on junk. Saying that was still too full of pain.

Conk had put her hands over her ears and was humming loudly, which was what she did when she didn't want to hear. She jammed her feet in her boots and backed out of the room, eyes flashing.

"Don't you *ever* talk that way 'bout him to me, you hear? I know who the mean one in *this* family is. You're just jealous 'cause we're happy together."

Conk walked out without even looking at Opie, without even taking her jacket, and called back over her shoulder just before she slammed the door, "You're just jealous 'cause you're so ugly, you'll *never* get a boyfriend."

The angry *click-click-click* of Conk's boots hit the stairs. Opie sank slowly down onto the bench in front of the vanity table and turned on the ruffled lamps. Leaning into the mirror, she counted the black freckles sprinkled like measles across her long brown face. Dull dead brown, she thought with disgust, the color of coffee with milk that had been sitting out on the table all day.

Ugly. Conk was right. She made a face at the skinny girl in the mirror. Suddenly she grabbed the hairbrush and began raking her hair back, pulling wildly through snarls that made her scream; brushing it flat, away, trying to make it disappear. When she looked in the mirror, the hair was still there, stiff as a corpse.

She took the scissors out of the drawer, slowly slipped her thumb and finger through the holes, and angrily snipped off a piece. It lay there on the plastic doily. She picked it up as if it were contaminated and hurled it into the trash can. Another hunk of dead, disgusting hair hit the trash, and another. Snip, snap, shorter and shorter, until stiff shards of frizzy hair poked out all over her head.

"Yuuuck!" she shouted at the mirror through clenched teeth. "I *hate* you!"

Suddenly she wanted to rip herself apart piece by piece— hair, skin, lips—let them lie there pitiful and quivering; wanted to start by scratching her face into a bloody pulp but her fingernails were bitten down beyond the quick. Then as she stared at her useless nails, the lights went out. It was delicate, how many air conditioners could get turned on at night before the old wiring short-circuited and they all had to light candles and miss their favorite TV programs.

Falling on her bed in the twilight, she curled up in a tight ball. A hand, it must have been hers, kept trying to yank the disgusting hair out by the roots. Hurt so bad she had to stuff the corner of the pillow into her mouth and scream. Then the hand froze up into a fist and started to beat her head and neck. It never seemed to be attached to her body when it did things like that—and it had done things like that a lot lately.

A long, low wail rumbled up from her belly and poured out of her throat as if a faucet had been turned on full force. Hot tears rolled down her cheeks, like poison from some ever-burning furnace inside. Opie wrapped the pillow around her face and cried, but no matter how long she cried, it always

17

seemed that she'd never be done with the sadness. Sadness stretched to the farthest end of her life like a dark, narrow alley with no way out.

Six months ago the same sadness had put fifty pure white aspirin tablets in the cup of her shaking hand. There on the edge of her bed, with radiators hissing and snowflakes falling down the air shaft, she'd watched a black pigeon flutter onto the windowsill as she took those pills. It had startled her with its orange, never-blinking eyes staring at her, moaning softly as it bent its neck down and up, down and up, then flew off, leaving little triangular tracks in the snow.

She had floated into thinking about white and black. White was a color she didn't know much about in this city where you grew up with in-between gray—white snow sucking up dirt wherever it landed, white marble stairs in the building always grimy, white underwear off the clothesline covered with soot.

But white was the color of the misty plain that opened out before her when she lay down that day on the pink-flowered quilt. Two months before she died, Grandma'am had taken her to get fabric for the quilt. Opie lay her cheek on a light pink square with bunches of blue violets in little woven baskets. That was a pattern Grandma'am had picked out special, since Grandma'am loved violets. Down in Georgia there were violets, she'd said, among the cottonwood trees, so many violets you could wade in them like water.

Opie had called softly to her grandmother, sensing her there in the deep mist as she drifted along the ceiling. Then her mother came running in. Don't shake me so, Ma'am, she'd tried to say. The woman had looked so forlorn that Opie just wanted to pull her up where everything was calm and they could see Grandma'am again.

The mist wasn't like New York fog—cold and tinged with gray; it was warm, with golden light shining through. Reach-

18

ing for the light, she'd noticed that there were hundreds of blackbirds soaring. Strange—those blackbirds in the white— but somewhere deep inside her she knew that behind the light there was dark, behind the white there was black, and it was good. Even while the *whee-ooop* of the ambulance had droned far away in her ears, the black was there keeping her safe.

Those pills never did much for Opie except give her a terrible stomachache she could still feel. Worst of all, they sent her poor mother to her knees. Since Grandma'am had died last year, her mother had depended on Opie to hold her up. That winter day the hardness in Opie's life had cracked wide open. Now she could barely hold onto her own life, let alone her mother's.

In the hospital where they flushed the mist out of her, her mother had sat on the foot of Opie's bed and sung every hymn she knew in her deep voice, rocking her thick body back and forth. When the woman couldn't think of any more songs, she'd brought up Brother Rasmus George from the A.M.E. Zion Church, who looked like a little brown speckledy toad and sang like one, too, and together they'd sung over Opie. Heal her broken spirit, they'd said. Nearly drove the other people in the hospital room out. Opie was so embarrassed she'd let her spirit be healed quickly just to shut them up.

Then when Opie had come home, Ma'am had left off singing and taken to sleeping the long hours of the day. Dr. Jamison had given her those pills to ward off her worrying, and she still swallowed them in big, hungry gulps.

Opie lay in the curve of her mattress for a long time in the gathering dark, not moving her cheek from the wet pillow, the ache in her chest heavy as a slab of concrete. Even without lights, the room was not quite dark and not quite quiet, just like the city. The roar of traffic stopped and started, then was drowned out by the rumble and screech of the subway vibrating the whole building. For a few seconds, the red light of an ambulance pulsed on the walls.

Out of the blankness a plan formed in Opie's mind and slowly pushed all the sadness back down where it could lie. Sitting up, she felt a thrill as she decided to spray paint a wall in the building, right under everyone's nose. No one would suspect her—Opal, the rock, the good girl. She smiled. She had cover.

Suddenly, she thought with a little thrill about the book of blank pages in her underwear drawer. For the first time in a year, she pulled the book out of the drawer. One day after school, about the time last year when she'd won a prize for an essay on Martin Luther King, Jr., her English teacher had handed her that book, saying, "Use it well now, Opal. You've got a real gift for writing." Even in the dark, the colors of the embroidered Chinese landscape on the cloth cover shimmered bright sapphire blue in her hands. "Use it well." What exactly did that mean? Scared her so much, she'd put the book in the back of her drawer and after a whole year there were only two unfinished poems in it.

She ran her fingers over its satiny smoothness. Its pages had a fresh smell all their own that fought the slightly vomity odor of the bedroom. She passed by the half-finished poems that were written neatly in English-teacher language, cracked open the spine on the fourth page, all smooth and snowy white, and waited. While she waited, words piled up inside her. Not words like the poems in some foreign English-teacher language. These words pressed so hard they didn't have time to get translated. These words were still in the language of her own heart.

Then the lights came on again, with an accompanying blare of TV laughter. Opie looked down at the blank page and wrote without hesitation:

20

My life ain't nothing but dirty brown. But I got something down in my soul come out of the white and it feels like a rainbow.

Sounded sort of like one of her mother's hymns, but she liked it.

This caged thing inside me roars to get out. I call it WILDCAT! and it is stronger than the streets, is stronger than this building. No one can catch it because it can fly!

THREE

Wildcat Uncaged!

A KEY RATTLED IN THE LOCK. It was her mother, home late from cleaning offices uptown. Opie had written pages and pages in the embroidered book, amazed at the words that poured out of her. She leaped quickly out of bed, shoved the book back in the drawer, jumped back in bed, and pulled the sheet up to her chin.

Her mother tiptoed through the kitchen to the living room and stood listening by the curtain that separated Frank's room. Frank was always out. Ma'am moaned softly and whispered something urgent to God as she came back into the room she and Opie shared. Opie pressed her eyes together as her mother bent over her bed, smelling of Lysol and sweat.

"Well, Lord, one chicken still home to roost," she sighed as she put on her nightgown and knelt down to have a talk with the Lord. The rusty whisper of her mother's voice filled the room for a long time. Probably praying about Georgia again, Opie thought. Lately Ma'am saw going back to Georgia as this family's salvation.

Grandma'am and Ma'am were born in Georgia. Grandma'am had been superintendent of this building for eighteen years before she'd finally saved up enough to go back down there last spring and visit her family. Three weeks later, Uncle Joro's voice on the phone said she had fallen sick real sudden and died.

Ma'am and Opie had gone down for the funeral. This place where her family was from, which she had imagined to be a shining city after listening to Grandma'am's stories, was not even a town—just ten or twelve gray shacks with rusted tin roofs set on a rise over the red-mud Willacoochee River.

Grandma'am had told her you could smell freedom there because that piece of bottomland had been given to her great-granddaddy and the other slaves on the Peel plantation long ago. What you could really smell was tobacco and poverty. Opie remembered the red dust kicking up a fuss, kudzu vines growing over everything that didn't move at least once a day, train whistle moaning so close it sounded like it would run right over your bed.

Now her mother's voice got all excited when she talked about how they could live in Georgia and how she'd get a good job at the mill. But Opie knew it was just one of those dreams they had stacked up on the shelves of their minds. Fact was they rarely had ten dollars left over after the month's expenses and that went to pay off Brother George, who had lent them every penny he'd saved to go home and mourn Queen Bess.

Opie listened for her mother's heavy breathing. Once asleep, her mother was a goner. This was Opie's special little blessing—it let her read late into the night and listen to her radio and was the next best thing to having her own room. She stared at the Glow-Ever hands of the radio clock as they inched past two. Frank came in. By two-thirty everything was quiet again.

She reached under the bed, pulled out the paint-can bag, and slipped into the dim, greenish glare of the hallway. The background roar from Houston Street was gone at this time of night. In the silence every creak sent her heart racing. She heard rustlings, the start of footsteps. No one came. The stairwell echoed back only emptiness.

The dull brown walls of the fourth floor were no good—big hole in the plaster by the stairs where she wanted to work. The third floor was dark—bulb out. On the second floor she stood staring at the wall, nervously rolling and unrolling the paint-can bag.

The metal balls inside the cans echoed like gunshot as she gently shook them. She popped off the cap, held the can straight out, drew in a deep breath, and pressed her finger down.

The spot of orange on the dirty wall looked like fire burning through from another world, edges shimmering like a star. The hiss of the can made the star explode! She began swinging her arm in wide arcs, like dancing in a dream. The bright ribbon of paint followed her every move. Back and forth, outline the letters in black, loop de loop, up and down, tuck them behind each other just like the pictures in her notebook. Wavy tiger stripes gave it real class. Out jumped the big, juicy word "WILDCAT!" It knocked her down.

She backed off, heady and faint from the paint fumes. It was no ordinary scribble—plain to see that. A rush of joy ripped through her, made her dance a lick and whirl around. There it was, out of the cage—"WILDCAT!" She wiped off a drip of paint with her T-shirt.

Then the iron police lock on someone's door clanged back. Her heart stopped. In three long steps she was up the stairs to the dark landing, pressed flat against the far wall, holding her breath.

"Oy vay!" came the drawn-out moan, then the *slap-slap* of slippers across the hall. Solomon Leshko! She felt more than doomed, she felt stupid. How you forget that old buzzard lives on the second floor? she asked herself. Marita Perez said he had the evil eye, the kind that sees through walls.

"Opal May Tyler, *what have you done?*" She cringed. He'd *seen* her! His voice was as loud as God's, piercing the dark-

24

ness of the landing like a hundred-watt bulb. Jerk was going to wake up the whole building for a little spray paint. She thought of running up to the roof, but her mind flashed on Solomon slapping upstairs, banging on her door, and waking her poor tired mother out of a dead sleep. That, and only that, made her set the paint cans silently on the landing and go down the stairs.

She stared at the top of the old man's bald head, pink and shiny under the bulb. She'd never seen it before. He always wore a hat, even in summer, but Opie knew a secret—he had on a black beanie under that hat. She had seen his beanie when she was in fifth grade. She and Conk had decided to find out, once and for all, if Solomon Leshko was a *brujo* witch, like Marita said, and if he went down to that Jewish place on Second Avenue and Houston Street every morning to put curses on all the rest of them in the building.

Opie had stood tottering on Conk's shoulder, staring in the open bottom of the tall window with a star on it. Solomon and a few old men with little black beanies and white capes were twirling strings around their heads and bobbing back and forth, muttering and howling like a pack of wolves. Up on the wall was some writing that had looked to Opie like a list of names. She'd squinted hard to see if there were names of anyone from their building, but they were all written in some kind of code.

Thank God he didn't sleep in that beanie, she thought on the next-to-last step. Probably couldn't jinx her without it, but she decided to run and cross herself, like Marita said, if he started bobbing.

He stood waiting at the bottom of the stairs, squinting up into the darkness at her. His fat stomach heaved in and out under his wine-colored bathrobe. He was wheezing and pulling with agitation on his white beard, which reached past the third button on his shirt when he was dressed. Now it was

25

smashed all over to one side like he'd been sleeping on it funny. A big old tomcat swished around his feet.

"So what's with this 'Wildcat!'?" he asked her in his heavy accent, waving his arm at her name on the wall. But he went right on, answered his own question. "All right. I wouldn't argue we live in a jungle. So what else is new? Now you have to make the announcement right outside my door?"

Opie suddenly felt nauseated from paint fumes.

"Uh, think I'm gonna be sick," she announced, clamping her hand over her mouth, trying to distract him long enough to get her mind back.

"Well, give to me the cans first, then I'll bring the mop," he replied undaunted, holding out his stubby hand. Opie went back up to the landing and took a long time in the dark, fumbling around to find the cans and trying to be sick to spite him.

"Your poor mother works 'til she drops to get off welfare and bring you up right," Solomon was babbling when she came back. "And now, it's down to the bottom of the barrel with all the rest." He illustrated her fall with a sharp downslide of his fist onto his hand. "You people are all the same." He shook his head slowly, wallowing in his disgust.

Hate crawled along her skin as she towered over him, gripping the paint cans, thinking, You're gonna get these cans all right—upside your head, old man.

"Your grandmother always told me"—amazing, she thought, he was still talking—"little Opal is different. So smart. Only four and already she reads. But I ask you—what is reading if it leads to this?" He was staring up at her from under his wild eyebrows, not noticing her white-hot anger. Idiot would pick three in the morning for conversation.

"I always tell them this place is no good for children anymore." Solomon was off on his social worker rap. "These days you children just stop trying. You don't care about nothing,

26

do you?" He sighed again more deeply and fell into another fit of wheezing. Opie watched him cough and struggle for breath.

"Sorry, Mr. Leshko," she said, making her voice sound small, the way she knew he wanted it to sound. Not sorry for a damn minute, she thought, but if anything would cut him short, an apology would be it.

Then she heard herself adding, "But sometimes you just gotta prove, you know, prove something. Make a mark somehow, like you'll be there tomorrow." Why did she say that to him? Never talked that way to anyone, even herself. Must be the silence.

Solomon reacted to her apology with complete surprise. He didn't say a word for ten whole seconds and clasped and unclasped his hands as if deep in thought.

"So that's why Frank killed the cat? To make a mark?" he asked finally. Solomon Leshko had hated her brother since the time he caught Frank wringing the neck of one of his beloved alley cats. His mouth curled up over his teeth as if he could eat Frank alive and spit out the bones.

Opie shrugged. "I don' know. Guess he just don't know how to let out his meanness."

"Well, never mind," he said. "I'll take this—and this"—he reached for the cans, holding each one up to examine it—"just in case I ever need to prove something myself. You never know." He looked at her like he was about to smile, but his eyes kept jumping to the top of her head. Opie reached up, suddenly remembering the short tufts of hair sprouting in all directions, and burst out laughing.

Solomon shuffled back toward his door, snorting and shaking his head. He touched the little metal box with a raging lion on the doorjamb and kissed his fingers like it gave him power or something. "Moishe, come," he called to the black-and-white cat, who stopped for a moment to fix its green eyes ac-

27

cusingly on her before it trotted in after him. The locks on his door went *click, clack, blam.*

She bit her lip. He'd tell Ma'am for sure—consider it his holy duty to upset her and scrape her daughter out of the bottom of the barrel.

Solomon was pretty tight with her mother. The day Ma'am had gotten off welfare, up he'd come to shake her hand—looked right over her mother's shoulder at Marita Perez, who happened to be sitting at their kitchen table. Man had barely turned around when Marita spat in the ashtray and said someone should accidentally shove that *mal Judío* off the roof.

What did the Jew know about welfare or any other kind of grief anyway? Opie thought, wiping the orange and black paint off her fingers onto her T-shirt. Didn't matter to him that the check her mother brought home was only twenty dollars more a month than welfare. Or that she never saw her children anymore, except on weekends, and then she was too tired to care much. Now, praise God, she was respectable in Solomon's eyes.

Ma'am never sassed Solomon behind his back like Marita and the others did. The old man had loved Queen Bess for some reason, and Ma'am respected him for that. When Ma'am had told him Grandma'am was dead, Solomon Leshko stood outside their door and sobbed like a baby. Embarrassed her mother half to death.

She sighed. When he squealed on her, she would see that look in her mother's eyes that said, "My God, how long do I have to keep on with this?" That look made Opie want to curl up on her bed with her head inside her knees and stay that way forever.

She gazed back at her new name leaping off the wall.

"Hey, old man, some people ain't got no eye for art," she said and made a face at his closed door, hoping he was still there, eye to the peephole. It felt deliciously good to be bad for once—to do something no one, not even she, expected.

28

FOUR

Wheel Without
a Hub

STRIPED MORNING CREPT INTO THE BEDROOM between the dusty slats of the venetian blind. Flopping over on her bed, chin in hand, Opie let go the edges of a dream where she had been huddled at the bottom of an air shaft. She smiled at her T-shirt with the orange and black smudges lying on the shag rug like a deflated balloon.

Over her bed was a big, bright-red Knicks poster; over her mother's a little gold-framed picture of Jesus smiling as if it pained him to do so. The aquamarine room felt dark and wet, kind of like an aquarium. Aquamarine made Opie want to barf, but it was the color Grandma'am had picked. They'd always lived in Grandma'am's apartment—the one the landlord had given her for being super of the building—and in these four rooms she had ruled the walls, the floors, the furniture, and the three of them. Grandma'am had always thought she knew more about you than you did and she often did.

But now the three of them were like a wheel without a hub. When Grandma'am died, this frayed family she'd kept patching over had begun to wear thin pretty quick, and the holes had gotten so big they wouldn't patch. Now Ma'am was taking little yellow pills, Frank was running wild on the streets, and she was fighting all the time just to live.

Opie got up on her knees and yanked the metal blind halfway up the window by her bed. Dust-filled light streamed across the pink quilt. She pushed up the screen and leaned out of the stale room to let the soft morning breeze brush over her face. Five floors below, the breeze rustled the leaves on the weedy Trees of Heaven that lined the chain-link fence around their building, growing through the shattered glass and concrete like a miracle. Sometimes she pretended they were palm trees on a desert island.

Her eyes drifted out over the tops of the cars in the parking lot next door to the back of the Palace hotel. It was where the Bowery winos slept. Through the open window she could see men in undershirts with their heads in their hands, sitting on cots set in long rows. A bell rang. The men in undershirts didn't move. Opie knew the hotel wardens would come in soon, yelling and pushing them out onto the street.

Five years ago Conk's building had stood in that parking lot. Then the city proclaimed Second Street an urban renewal site and Conk and her mom moved to the apartment upstairs from Opie. One day a wrecking crane ten stories tall came rumbling up the street. A big lead ball swung out over the rooftops—*KAVOOM!* Brick walls crumbled into dusty heaps, showing the insides of rooms and stairs climbing to nowhere.

No one in the neighborhood thought much anymore about what had been there before, except maybe Solomon Leshko. But people stayed in because there weren't any stoops to sit out on and because their friends had gone to the projects over on Avenue D.

She pulled down the screen and walked into the bathroom. In the toothpaste-spattered mirror, the results of last night's hair chopping took her breath away. Leaning on the sink, she felt stomach-sour and hopeless. Bad enough to be ugly and de-formed *with* hair, but without it . . . *gross!*

After growling and pacing around like a caged animal, Opie

30

decided there was only one thing that could save her. She got the scissors and began to cut again, this time carefully, shorter and shorter, until the hair was a woolly Afro. Staring at the shape of her head, feeling the air cool her scalp, she thought, Maybe this gonna be okay somehow. Never knew she had such a long neck. She put on her dangly silver earrings and swung them back and forth, lost in the motion and newness of it all.

After her shower, she got a hair pick and walked into the bedroom, raking. She put on a tight pink tank top. In the vanity mirror, her breasts were little buds poking out of her telephone pole body. Bruises from where she had beaten herself last night ringed her neck. She started to take the top off, sighed, and pulled it back down.

In the kitchen, she opened the fridge, grabbed wildly for the orange juice while holding her breath, and closed the door, all in one motion. Since yesterday the sour smell had gotten so bad it made her eyes water. Opie hated to clean the fridge and her mother slept so much these days that she never noticed the forest of smelly green mold taking over in there.

The clock above the table clicked past eight-thirty. She set down the juice carton and went into the living room, where the wide arch into Frank's room was covered with a flowered curtain that Grandma'am had made out of old drapes.

"Frank," she called, ear to the closed curtain. "You gotta get to work by nine."

Absence of sound. Just like all the rotten school mornings when the scuzhead refused to get up. Since her mother had been working nights, Opie's charge had been to see that Frank was in an upright position before she left for school.

Now that he'd turned sixteen, he'd sworn this school year would be his last. If Grandma'am had been there, she would have put her hands on her hips and said: "Ain't no one in this fam'ly gon' quit on something they start. Franklin, y'all done

31

started school and y'all gonna finish it!" Frank could never argue with her.

But Ma'am could beg him not to quit, even tear her heart out and lay it on the table, all bloody and beating. Frank just dumped it in the trash and walked away. Then Opie had to tell Ma'am to stop crying, everything gonna be all right. But they both knew different.

"Get up, you jerk!" she yelled over her shoulder, turning the TV on loud because she knew it bothered him. Retreating to the kitchen, she pushed the last two pieces of bread down in the toaster and wiped the counter where the roaches had been feasting on spilled bean juice and jam.

"Do I care if he make his probation job?" she muttered to herself, daring to open the fridge briefly for the butter. "Let 'em throw him in the slam. Solve a shitload of problems."

The TV clicked off. As the half-burned toast popped up, Frank's image slumped silently across the toaster. He pulled open the fridge door and got a can of beer.

"Whew!" His face screwed up as he slammed it shut. "Load this thing in a hearse and take it over to Serotti's quick!"

Opie laughed. "Yeah, good idea—they give it a funeral and I won't hafta clean it."

Frank swung his leg over the back of the chair and sat down at the gray Formica table. He rolled the cold beer can across his forehead, then slapped it down on top of a cockroach and let his head sag heavily on his bare chest. A blue tattooed snake wound round and round his arm from his wrist to just below his shoulder. She remembered how Ma'am had cried for two days and refused to get out of bed when she saw that snake. Long hair fell in shiny black waves over his strong shoulders. She'd always wanted hair like Frank's. Her mother kept saying not to worry, Opie had more *under* her hair than Frank had, but it never made things better, being smart.

His handsome face was gray and empty, eyes fixed somewhere far off like he'd been wrestling with death and only half won. She looked away, wondering what it was he had done last night to get so wasted.

She poured juice, buttered the overdone toast, and threw it on a plate in front of him. He gave her a sour look and shoved the plate away. She sat down across from him.

"Hey, man, am I your mother?" she asked, bravely taking a bite of her own charcoal toast.

"Lord, Thy mercy prevaileth yet!" He rolled his eyes heavenward in a perfect imitation of Grandma'am rising to preach out of the front pew of the Zion Church. Opie giggled. If only he'd make them laugh more these days, instead of making them cry.

His hands trembled as he lit his cigarette and popped open the beer can. Then he folded his arms and looked at her like she was some sort of deformed monster.

"You tried swinging on trees yet?" he asked and laughed wildly like he'd made some kind of joke. Then he reached over and poked at one of the painful bruises around her neck. "Hey, guess I'd wanna kick my own ass, too, if I looked like a damn ape."

"Shut up," she said, brushing crumbs off the table. She was used to his put-downs. "Hey listen, jerk, I sprayed a wall—downstairs."

Frank's eyes narrowed. "Microbrain. Landlord pin the rap on me and you know it."

"Nah. Check this out." Opie giggled. "There I am blasting away on that wall in the middle of the night. Out comes Leshko in his pajamas and man, was he jumping up and down. I thought he'd bust a vessel and die right there in the hall!" Frank looked up with the shadow of a smile. He loved anything that tortured Solomon.

"Girl, you a real fox." He slid her a warm sideways look, like he did with the girls on Fourth Street, and gave her his playful punch, which was always too hard. For a moment time rolled back and he was the same Frank who had protected her from Striker Jackson, the bully who used to live on the third floor when they were little; same Frank who had built forts out of cardboard boxes with her in the jumble of Paradise Alley behind the building. She wished with all her heart she could bring that other Frank back. Now his body lived with them, but he was behind a wall that got higher every day.

"Got a line on Leshko," Frank mused to himself, twisting the gold cobra ring with ruby eyes around his finger the way he always did when his mind was working overtime.

Opie's heart caught on the barbed tone in Frank's voice. Leave that old man alone, she almost said, and then wondered why she should care. Let Frank make the Jew's life unbearable, so maybe he'd move away and leave the building to the rest of them. But one thing kept coming at her like a bullet in the chest. Old man was right. Frank should never have killed that cat. Now that she thought about it, the cat turned out to be the beginning. Her brother saw he could get away with letting out his mean. But Solomon didn't understand about feeling mean. Frank's face clouded up, as if he'd read her thoughts, and he blew smoke in her face because he knew she hated it.

"You skunk!" she said, holding her breath and waving the smoke away. "Conk just too young and stupid to smell what you *really* are."

Frank laughed. "Maybe she finally got better things to do than hang out with Miss Ugly America."

"Well, if *you* the one she hanging out with, sure be sorry business."

"Butt out, baby, 'less you wanna get hurt big-time."

"Oh, I am so scared. See me shake?" She held out her hand.

Frank stood up, knocking over his chair. She ducked his fist.

"Don't touch me, scumbag!" she shouted, hurling her dish into the sink. It shattered on top of the unwashed plates from the night before and the night before that.

She hardly heard Frank growl about tying her ugly mouth together. Each step away from him felt springy, catlike, free. No use in getting angry with Frank anymore. You'd end up wearing your life away and he'd do whatever he wanted anyway. Might as well leave your anger broken to pieces in the kitchen sink.

She got her embroidered book off the night table. Her mother lay facing the wall, facing her little Jesus picture, snoring away. Opie sighed. Adjusting the vanity mirror up, she stepped back, uncurling her shoulders. Better to be tall, she thought. Models were supposed to be six foot. Might be almost six foot next year. 'Course models ain't got no rock-hard muscles in their shoulders and legs, but models ain't living on Second Street either. Here you gotta be strong, ready to jump. She raised her chin and flung back her shoulders. Pink tank top looked okay after all. Almost made her look like a girl. She blotted out the static of Frank's voice in her brain. Ugly or not, ain't got nothing to hide. That boy was not going to pull her down with him.

As she walked out of the apartment door, she barely saw Frank still standing beside the table, his clenched fists ready, his face full of clouds.

&

FIVE

Wildcat
Rescued

SITTING ON THE GRITTY MARBLE STAIRS in the second-floor hall, Opie listened uneasily for stirrings in Solomon Leshko's apartment but decided he must be down at the place on Second Avenue muttering. Soft light filtered through the blue, orange, and green panes of the hall window, giving her a whole new perspective on her wall. She opened the embroidered book across her knees and made a shaded drawing of her name, "WILDCAT!"

Already the rolling beat of reggae pounded up out of Claude, the super's, apartment. He had taken over cleaning the building when Grandma'am left last spring. Opie knew that when Solomon Leshko banged on his door complaining about the new graffiti, Claude would nod his head about painting it over and then do nothing. He hated the old man about as much as Frank did, maybe more.

Solomon used to argue with Claude about the filthy water he slopped over the hall floors and go on about how Queen Bess Tyler had worn her knees out scrubbing the marble as white as the stairway to heaven. One day the old man washed a clean place in front of the mailboxes so everyone could see what kind of job this new super was doing. Claude had waited for the old man to get his mail, then asked him if he knew anything about that little white spot. Solomon had started sniffing around again and Claude went right over the edge and drew out a knife. Only thing that stood between Solomon Leshko and certain death was the old man's lungs and Big Mario, who'd heard the commotion and come rushing out.

She took a deep breath and let the power of the name surge right down into her and out across the page of her book.

Strong! Mighty. Pow! WILDCAT! They all be busy building cages, but she's too smart, this WILDCAT! No cage can hold her long. Don't dream too big. Just keep waking up every morning, looking out the bars, working on wings to fly. When I learn to use those wings someday soon, ain't no one gonna drag me down.

Down the stairs behind her came Conley, the blonde social worker who sat closest to the window at the storefront housing office on Second Avenue. Opie stood up. Conley was seriously studying her wall. "Glad to see someone thought of painting the halls," she said with a laugh. She been talking up a rent strike against the landlord if he didn't fix the building. She hadn't lived there too long and still thought every problem had a solution if only people got together.

Opie giggled and looked down, nervous and off balance. She put a casual hand over the bruises on her neck. Being around Conley scared her. Didn't even know her first name. Queen Bess had always called the new people by their last names because that was the way they were down on the rent list.

"Hey Opie, you working this summer?" Conley asked.

"Ain't found nothing yet. Gotta be sixteen mostly."

"Well, we got the okay from the city to open a recreation center for the Bowery men—right next to the mission soup kitchen. Sure could use your help with cleaning and painting."

Pretty lady, Conley, Opie thought. Long golden hair, like a

37

princess in a book. Didn't never seem to be no princesses with kinky black hair.

"When you want me to start?"

"Come on over Monday morning. I'll be there." Conley smiled up at Opie as she walked on down the stairs. "Hey, your hair looks great!"

Opie's mouth dropped open. "Huh?"

"I mean it," Conley called up as she fiddled with her broken mailbox. "Really brings out your face. You've got good bones."

Bones. Opie felt her face. Well, at least someone had a use for her, maybe would treat her with a little respect. Conley was always trying overhard to be super nice to poor people. Opie figured since she was a social worker, that was her job.

No sooner had she sat down again and begun to write, when who should labor up the stairs and stand staring at her and her name on the wall but Solomon Leshko. Short and round as an egg, he had black suspenders over a yellowing white nylon shirt, and on top of his head sat that black beanie again, perched between the tufts of hair over his ears. His overgrown eyebrows looked like fire burning. And he did *not* look pleased.

"Uh, my mother, she's sleeping now, Mr. Leshko," she said quickly to deflect him from marching her upstairs to tell her mother what a rotten, bottom-of-the-barrel girl she had turned into.

"Your mother? I need *you*," he said. Man, this was even worse.

"Me?" Nothing in her life would follow along anymore. It filled her with dread.

"Is there someone else around?" he asked with mock seriousness, lifting his chin to look over her shoulder.

She glanced under her arm, playing his game temporarily, but set on escape.

38

"Nope."

"Well . . . ? I guess you'll have to do."

Opie swallowed, not daring to ask, Do *what?* He started down the stairs.

"Opal?" he called up, obviously expecting her to follow. She hesitated, kicking herself for getting into this. Maybe if she helped him he'd keep his big mouth shut, she thought, as she followed him downstairs into the air shaft courtyard.

"*Oy,* have we got problems today," he said, bending over with a groan to right an overturned dish of cat food and pick up an undershirt that had fallen off someone's clothesline. "That Romeo, the bum, he's eating the kittens in the cellar. I want you to help me save the poor little one left."

Romeo was the dirty orange tom responsible for the population explosion among the alley cats that had caused Solomon, their self-appointed protector, so many problems. Solomon worried over those cats winter and summer. They starved—he spent his Social Security money for cat food. They got their ears ripped off—he patched them up. They abandoned their kittens—he took them in.

Solomon pushed the metal trash cans away from the building and pointed to a less-than-person-sized hole in the foundation. He looked up at her as if she climbed into dark, rat-infested cellars every day.

"No way I'm going in there," she said, thinking he really *was* out of his mind, like Rosie said.

"It was crouching just inside when I looked before. Come see," he said, gesturing as if he hadn't heard her.

He got down on his hands and knees with a grunt and shined a flashlight into the hole. She knelt obediently on the cracked concrete beside him and looked in where he was pointing. Sure enough, not two feet from the hole, there was something on the dirt, backed up against the wall.

"All the rest he's killed, every one. I scared him off until we could get this one."

"Just a stupid alley cat, Mr. Leshko," Opie pointed out, standing up and dusting off, ready to leave.

"Stupid alley cats don't like to die any more than you." He backed away from the hole on all fours.

"You said it, man. I don't like to die."

"Not to worry, Opal. Only a tiny little cat, is all."

"Yeah, and about a thousand rats."

"So? That's why we need the cats!" He spread his hands dramatically. "You are its only hope. Think about that poor little one when Romeo comes back."

"Oh, chill out," she said, grabbing the flashlight and thinking this had *better* even them up about the wall.

The top of her body barely fit through the hole sideways. She lunged in the direction the creature had been and prayed that the furry thing in her hand was actually a cat and not something else. Whatever it was let out a piercing howl and began wildly thrashing, biting and clawing her hand into a bloody pulp. She shot back through the hole and threw it against the fence. Solomon picked it up and began dabbing at her hand with a snotty handkerchief. Outraged, Opie walked away, but he followed and lodged himself between her and the door.

"Wait just a minute! You see, I can't take this cat," he said. "You know Josephine next door to me—how she complains, complains about my cats. Last week she called the landlord, so I promised her, on my honor, no more cats. You could take it for a few days 'til old Sol finds a home, right?" Why did he care so much about these flea-bitten animals?

"My mother, she hates cats," Opie said, "and man, she'd *really* hate that cat."

She eyed the bony bundle of matted orange fur huddled against Solomon's shirt as she held her throbbing, bloody hand in the air. It stared defiantly back at her with one runny blue eye—the other one was closed shut and full of pus.

"Let old Sol talk to your mother." He wouldn't stop. That was his major problem, pushing until people caved in or tried to kill him, one or the other.

"Look, promise not to tell about last night?" she asked, deciding to drive the bargain now that the stakes were getting so high.

Solomon's face fell into a relieved smile.

"What's to tell? Only a *khazer* would tell, no?"

He held the animal up and lifted the skinny tail just long enough to say, "It's a girl!" before the kitten turned on him, snarling.

"Now, now, Bubeleh, what *chutzpah!* You be a nice girl."

He was actually talking to the cat as if she were human. Opie had never been around anyone with pets, except her Uncle Del in Georgia, who talked to his old yellow dog with the heel of his shoe.

He poked around at the cat's stomach. The immediate result was a hiss that would have made a snake proud.

"*Oy.* She's starving already for days, eh, Bubeleh?" He rubbed his nose on the kitten's dirty pink one. She put a tiny paw on his cheek but didn't resist. "Feed her a little milk, a little honey, a little egg, mixed up—like so."

Solomon held the cat out in the palm of his hand.

"Take her like this," he instructed, pinching the nape of her neck and holding her out like a sack of onions. Opie pinched her neck above Solomon's fingers, held the cat out at arm's length, and walked swiftly through the building door.

"Little Bubeleh, she is a special one, Opal. I just feel it," Solomon called after her, his hand on his heart. "And you have done a great *mitzvah* for her, praise God."

* * *

41

Unlocking the door with a whirling wild cat in hand was like jumping double-dutch with one leg tied up. She opened the door a crack, threw the cat inside, and squeezed in behind her just as the cat sprinted back out into the hall. She finally cornered the dumb thing on the fourth floor, lunged for the nape of her neck, bolted up the stairs, and hurled the struggling furball onto the living room couch. The kitten momentarily stared at Opie with her runny eye before skittering under the black vinyl chair, where she barricaded herself with loud growls and hisses.

Opie gave up and walked into the kitchen, turned on the faucet, and let the water run over her bloody, aching hand. She was glad, for once, that Ma'am was sleeping. Maybe she could keep the kitten a secret. Ma'am was usually only out of bed a few hours before she left to go up to Madison Avenue and clean. On weekends she stumbled around wrapped in her bathrobe and her worryings, except for Sunday mornings, when she went to the church.

The milk was on the verge of turning, they were out of eggs, and honey was not something they ever bought, but Opie didn't dare leave to go shopping until her mother was safely on her way to work. She poured a bowlful of milk, then searched everywhere for the cat, wiggling around on the floor to see under places that hadn't been cleaned since Grandma'am had left.

The little stinker was nowhere. Opie stared at the always-closed curtain that served as a divider between the living room and Frank's room. Frank warned them weekly that if he ever caught them in there, they were dead meat. Said he had booby traps all set. But the stupid cat had picked his room to hide out in.

She slipped inside and lifted the covers of Frank's bed off the floor. Underneath, on top of a lumpy pink towel shoved toward the back, sat Miss Pee Wee. Opie lay down and started

42

inching cautiously under the bed. Pee Wee watched her, then simply backed farther out of reach.

Opie gave up and lay with her chin on her hands, looking at that towel. There were any number of illegal and dangerous things that her brother might want to hide, she knew that. But when she lifted the corner of the towel, she wished she hadn't. It was his store of weapons—half a dozen switchblades, a pistol, a strange-looking lead club with a leather thong, and a coil of heavy orange rope with hooks and harnesses. Quickly she rearranged the towel over the pile.

She put the bowl of milk near the bed and sat, cross-legged.

"Hey, Pee Wee, this boy *kills* little kitties like you, believe me." Reason didn't work any better than spoiled milk.

Opie decided to wait the cat out. Seemed like her life, which in go-along times stayed just beyond her reach, was breaking apart into pieces, none of which could be fit back together. Suddenly she longed for the familiar ache of life before yesterday.

Pee Wee finally peeked out, and soon her tiny pink tongue was flicking madly, lapping up the milk. Smiling at her success, Opie watched the scrawny thing drain the bowl and sit back, awkwardly cleaning her dirty face with her paw. When the kitten suddenly jumped a foot in the air sideways and landed on a dust ball, Opie burst out laughing. The cat rolled around with the dirty socks and finally ended up inside one of Frank's shoes, from which she leaped on an unsuspecting roach.

"Way to go, Pee Wee!" cheered Opie, clapping her hands and giggling. This was fun—first fun she'd had in weeks.

Opie sat on the sofa gently scrubbing the feather-soft, copper-colored fur and wiped the cat's disgusting eyes with a wad of wet paper towels, which made the little thing look more like a drowned rat than a cat. Then she held the damp body against her skin, just above her tank top, and slowly became aware of a vibration on her chest. Pee Wee was purring, rattling so that every inch of her shook as she curled up against Opie and went to sleep. Opie sat very still, almost not breathing. She followed every delicate little orange tiger marking, stroked the whiskers, peeked into the pearly pink ears, and had to keep herself from squealing for joy.

Clumsily, keeping the curled cat like a baby on her shoulder, she walked into the bedroom, got out her embroidered book, and went back into the living room to write:

Tamed a wild cat today. Or maybe she tamed me. Funny how last night I wrote our name on the wall. She's so soft and little and quiet lying here. But this scratched-up hand of mine shows how ferocious she is inside. She wants a piece of life, just like I do. Where we gonna find it, Pee Wee?

SIX

❦

The Violet
China Plate

AT NOON HER MOTHER WAS STILL SLEEPING like a dead woman. Opie put the cat on the chair, then went through every drawer and cabinet in the kitchen—not a single clean plate or fork! There were dishes in the sink, dishes on the counter, cups with coffee dregs everywhere, bowls with spoiled milk and Cocoa Pops. The mess looked the way this family felt.

Sighing, she fished out of the sink the broken shards of the plate she had hurled across the kitchen that morning and set them together on the counter. Like a puzzle, she pushed the pieces next to one another, toward the center. Sad—that plate was part of Grandma'am's set of violet Sunday china, white with light brown crackles and little faded blue violets twining around the edge. Now it would never go together again—like so many things. She left the pieces lying on the counter and piled the everyday yellow plastic plates around them.

Opie scrubbed and dried three drainer loads of dishes, stacking them neatly behind the glass cabinet doors, hanging all the cups on Grandma'am's hooks. She scrubbed the worn-out Con-Tact paper on the counter and swept a dustpan full of dirt from the floor. In her head she heard her grandmother's voice: "If you gon' do a job, do it right now, chile." Opie smiled. Then the springs on her mother's bed squawked!

She ran back into the living room, where Pee Wee was still

45

sleeping peacefully on the black vinyl chair, and piled two pillows carefully in front of the cat. The toilet flushed; then came the dry scrape of bare feet on the kitchen floor and water shushing into the coffeepot. The cat yawned, exposing tiny white points of teeth, and put her head back down on her paws. Cereal slid into a bowl.

"Opal."

"Ma'am."

"You the one broke this violet plate?"

"Sorry." She'd forgotten she left it pieced together there by the sink.

"Come clean it up, girl."

Ma'am didn't seem to notice the spotless kitchen. She sat at the table in her nightgown and the plaid scarf she always wore to bed. Head leaning on her hand as if her body couldn't hold her up, she stared at the coffee in front of her like it was the last thing on earth she could imagine drinking.

Opie slid quietly into the seat across the table. Her mother sighed. Defeat lived deep in the lines along the side of Ma'am's mouth lately and Opie knew that, under the closed eyelids, her eyes were dull with the thought of another day.

She wondered if her mother was dreaming again about Fish Boy Harmon. He wasn't a boy anymore, but a pot-bellied man, who fished for catfish in the Willacoochee River. Opie had met him at Grandma'am's funeral. After they'd come back, he had written Ma'am a misspelled letter printed in pencil that started, "Cum on back, my sweet batooty." Her mother had made her read the letter out loud. So Opie knew that when she talked about going back to Georgia, her mother's mind was really hooked on Fish Boy.

"Tell me 'bout Fish Boy, Ma'am," she asked, for the first time.

"What you wanna know 'bout him for?" Ma'am snapped, suddenly coming alive.

46

"Guess I wanna know 'bout you."

Her mother laughed a private little laugh. "Oh, he just someone I know."

"You like him, don't you?"

"Girl, you bad. Shut up, you hear?" Ma'am was trying to be tough, but there was a smile starting at the corners of her mouth.

"Ain't bad to like someone. Tell me 'bout him." Opie smiled back.

"What you wanna know stuff for? Just stuff, that's all."

"You never tell me nothing 'bout you, Ma'am."

"Oh Lord, Opal, you like a big ole vulture waiting to pick me apart."

"You wrong, Ma'am. Got me mixed up with Queen Bess." Ma'am looked at her a long time, like a whole scene was passing before her eyes.

"So how old was you when you met him?" Opie asked.

"Well, guess it all started when I'se 'bout your age. Boy always fishing, day and night. I'd come 'round the wharf to buy catfish and Lord, you could see the white fly up in that boy's eyes. One night, I put on my Sunday dress and climbed right out the window. There he was, down by the dock, dark-fishing in the river. Next day Queen Bess say, 'Where you get all them big red 'skeeter bites?' But I just told her there's a big ole hole in my screen."

Her mother rolled her eyes and giggled like she was fourteen again. Opie giggled, too. Felt like they were girlfriends for the first time.

"I loved that boy up and down. He was good to me like no one else. Then I got to watching the whites of Queen Bess's eyes getting kinda narrow when we's setting together on the porch. Your granddaddy long dead by then and my brothers all grown up. I knew Queen Bess reckoned I needed tending and the name of that tending was away—fast!

47

"Now 'long 'bout that time my brother Del set his mind on a New York City job, so he starts out for the bus station early one morning, and there we was, Bess and me, hoisting our suitcases up on our shoulders. I walked in front of Queen Bess, bawling all the way."

Ma'am stopped.

"Tell the rest. What about here?" Opie said, hoping Ma'am would get to *her* father.

"You don' wanna hear the rest, sugar. Just goes down from there."

"Wanna hear it *all*, Ma'am. Every little piece."

"Lord, I don't know. Bess got the super job through the church. Del got discouraged pretty quick and he's off to the army. I bawled straight on through the winter. All them cars and people and lights got me so deep-down scared, just wanna go back and set on the bank again watching that old red river. Honey, I can't tell no more."

"Tell 'bout Ellis Lee, Ma'am?" Opie's heart was pounding.

"Don't wanna talk 'bout Ellis Lee, you hear?"

"Please, Ma'am. I got a right to know."

Her mother sighed a big, chesty sigh and was quiet so long Opie got worried that she might back off.

"Humph. This some can of worms crawling all over."

Opie chewed her already-chewed thumbnail and begged Ma'am with her eyes. She could feel the hunger growing inside her.

"That man near six and a half feet tall, like some giant. Had kinda laughing-type eyes, not pretty, but sorta dragging you in close.

"Queen Bess say, 'Boy, you work for a living?' 'fore she even let him set his rear on her sofa.

"But Ellis Lee got all the right answers, so we set long hours on that sofa just laughing it up. But he didn't like Frank. Say Frank look like a white baby. Told him 'bout Chico being

48

half Puerto Rican, but he didn't wanna hear it. Man had worked hisself up to a job driving the oil truck all over the Lower East Side, and he had him a little apartment up on Fourteenth Street. I knowed a steady thing, so I went to staying in his apartment, fixing it up for him, and leaving Frank with Bess."

Ma'am stopped again and played with the spoon. She sighed. "Just after you's born, that man gone. Come back once to see his little girl when you's two; say he in night school, gonna make something of hisself. Then off he goes. Queen Bess so mad she march on up to Fourteenth Street to roust that boy out, but he moved and no one knew where. Never knew how to keep a man."

Opie got up and put her arms around her mother's shoulders. "You pretty, Ma'am. And you smart, too. Only thing, you don't know it."

"Gotta get a education, Opal. Never was too good at figuring. Can't hardly read. Minute we come to New York, I'se helping Bess with the building. Had to quit school." Her mouth went slack.

Opie's mind was reeling, trying to digest the scraps of information her mother had let out about her father. Suddenly Ma'am grabbed her face.

"Your mother deep down prouda having a daughter got real brains, win that English prize. You stay in school, you hear? Don't let some scumbag little boy give you no baby he ain't never gonna look at again. You *hear?*" Her mother had started shaking her until her teeth rattled. Opie wrenched herself free.

"Don't worry, Ma'am. No scumbag little boy *ever* gonna like *me* that much."

"Aw, hon, you just late blooming," her mother said, taking her hand, "but when you do, you not gonna believe it. Sometime I think growing up more in your mind, Opal. Happen when you decide you okay."

Her mother's eyes started probing the living room. Opie caught her breath, trying to see if Pee Wee was rolling around with dust balls again.

"Opal." It sounded ominous. "What happen to your hair?" Opie smiled, relieved. "Cut it."

"Cut it? Might as well shave you head, be one of them Hare Krishna. That fuzz make you look like a boy."

"You wrong. This fuzz make me look like a black girl."

Ma'am sighed and reached over to feel the top of her daughter's head.

"Frank get on down to his job?" she asked.

"Don' know." Opie wasn't going to lie for him anymore.

The line between her mother's eyes deepened as she looked over at Opie. She lifted a shaking hand to her forehead.

"Ma'am, don't start," Opie begged.

"If he don't make that probation job, he be in big trouble." Ma'am began to sob and shudder as she rose and turned toward the bedroom. Opie darted over, blocking the door into the hallway.

"Don't go back in there," she pleaded, thinking again about flushing those little yellow pills down the toilet. "You can't talk to no pillow."

"Get more talk outa that pillow than I get outa you and your brother combined these days." Her mother dropped heavily back into the chair, tears running down her cheeks. Opie hugged her from behind, angry again at Frank for being such a jerk.

"What I got if I ain't got my children?" Ma'am wailed and leaned her wet cheek against Opie's hand. "Can't stop me from grieving. Got one on the street and one end up near dead from hating herself."

"Ma'am, I told you. Ain't gonna *do* that again."

"All I know is I done teached you what I know. Done teached you Jesus. Done teached you doing unto others. Ya'll

sure turn *that* one round fast! Maybe I don't know nothing."
Her mother looked up at the ceiling as though she was writing
an overdue notice for services rendered to the Almighty.

Opie took out the pick she'd put in her pocket that morning,
untied her mother's scarf, and combed gently through the frizzled strands. Combing opened up a sad place in Opie's chest,
made her remember Grandma'am. Sometimes they'd sit together for hours, Queen Bess parting and combing and braid-
ing the cornrows and talking about the people in the building
and the Willacoochee flood and Jesus and all the other things
she talked about.

Suddenly her mother grabbed Opie's hand and kissed it
hard. "You a good girl, Opal. You even clean the kitchen.
What I do without you?"

❧

SEVEN

A Place To Hide

OPIE SAT CROSS-LEGGED ON THE FLOOR of the dark living room after her mother left, the cat curled on her knee, her mind fixed like a magnet on Ellis Lee.

Over and over she imagined herself walking up to a fine stucco house in Yonkers with emerald green grass. She'd knock on the door and there he'd be—giant-tall and handsome, smiling like, was she some Girl Scout selling cookies? Then his eyes would get wide and he'd know her. She'd fall into his arms and he'd hold her tight. Never been held tight by a man, ever, she thought. It set off a hunger in her too deep for words.

The breeze from the window fan played with the open pages of the embroidered book on the coffee table. She sighed as she ran her hand along the little bumps and grooves of her pen marks on the paper. Sadness started seeping back in under the edges of the power she'd been feeling.

Suddenly she caught her breath. The locks on the apartment door fiddled open and she heard Frank talking to someone. Opie pulled the kitten close to her chest. Her brother's heavy step in the kitchen was followed by the light *click, click* of high heels. It was Conk! Silently she inched over beyond the sofa, half behind the end table, and sat, hoping they would go away.

The sour refrigerator smell drifted in. Frank slammed the fridge door shut, making a big deal. Loud giggling, definitely Conk's. Opie's heart pounded. Someone popped open two beer cans, then struck a match and inhaled. Slowly the sweet smell of pot replaced the refrigerator smell.

"I got my sister trained," Frank said confidently, as if carrying on from an earlier conversation. "She won't rat on us, baby. She knows I'd break her arm."

"I don't trust her," Conk said, squirming so that her bottom squeaked on the vinyl chair. "Girl is so busy minding everyone else's business. God, I hate saints, never got no business of their own."

Frank inhaled again and held his breath while he spoke. "Well, baby, *you* broke this open. Why you let her see us?"

"Man, I tried to shake her. She's worse than my little sister."

Opie bit her lip hard as the tears pushed up in her throat and spilled over. This was her best friend?

"Well, dreamboat, she buzzing 'round like a hornet 'bout us—*mmmm*—so we gotta be—*mmm*—foxy," came Frank's smothered voice. A chair scraped back. Her brother was probably kissing Conk's neck. Opie was sure of it when she heard Conk moan. Another chair scraped back. Several minutes of silence followed, full of heavy breathing, rustling, smacking, and little "oo's" from Conk.

By the time they came through the living room they were a moving embrace. Frank's shirt was gone. Conk's shirt was around her shoulders. Their bodies rocked back and forth while he steered her in an expert dance through the curtain, kissing her passionately all the while.

So that was how he did it, Opie thought through her tears, remembering bitterly all the afternoons since Ma'am had started working when she'd stayed locked in her room while Frank "entertained."

53

There was an explosion of panting and moaning on the squeaky bed. Opie grabbed her book and blindly stumbled out of the living room, knocking into the chair they'd left in the middle of the kitchen. They didn't even hear.

Out in the hall her heart sank as she remembered Pee Wee. The cat must have climbed out of her lap. Nothing but Pee Wee could have made her go back. She put down her book carefully by the door, stuck her fingers in her ears, and ran through the apartment as if she were holding her breath underwater. The pulse of moans had risen to an unbearable pitch. Desperately, she felt around the floor and couch, throwing pillows, nearly upsetting the lamp. Finally under the chair, her hand grasped the furry body, just as the sounds in the other room stopped!

Opie froze, then turned her head slowly toward the curtain. Frank came through, struggling to put on his pants. Opie bolted over the coffee table and lunged for the kitchen door, but he spread his arms over it.

"What the *hell* are you doing here?" he asked, glowering.

She stepped back, trying to slide the cat behind her, but he saw the motion and grabbed her arm. She pulled it away from him and put a trembling hand over Pee Wee.

"Aw, a sweet little kitty," he simpered, a demon light growing in his eyes. "Lemme see."

He ripped the cat away, dangling her by the tail in front of his face. Pee Wee flailed helplessly in the air. Like a fire, the memory of the kitten he'd killed burned through her mind. Over and over that cat had dropped from his fist in her dreams, dropped like a rag doll that was really a bomb exploding inside her chest.

The fingers of his hand closed around Pee Wee's tiny neck.

"NO!—NO!—NO!" Opie heard herself yell. With a tameless towering fury, she threw herself against her brother, glad for once that she was almost as tall as he was. Surprised and

54

off guard, he fell backward onto the kitchen floor, still holding the cat. She leaped on top of him, her hands circling his neck, banging his head wildly against the linoleum, thumbs shoving his Adam's apple into his windpipe. He grunted, straining to get up, struggling to keep the cat in one hand while his other pushed at her face, flattening her nose so she couldn't breathe.

For a long moment they held each other off. She heard Conk's hysterical screaming behind her, felt fists raining down on her shoulders, then long nails digging into her chest. In a frenzy of strength, Opie kicked at Conk and pushed down on Frank's neck until his red, writhing face turned purple and the rage in his eyes widened into fear. His body convulsed as he threw the cat against the wall. Opie lunged for the animal and ran like a shot out the door. As she scooped up her book, she heard her brother's moaning and Conk's hysterical voice:

"*Querido, ay* darling, you okay? I swear I'll *kill* her!"

"Leave that to me," Opie heard Frank croak.

Her feet barely touched the marble stairs, down and around, down and around, to where? She leaned against the front door, heart pounding so hard it shook her whole body, and listened for his footsteps on the stairs. What if he called the police and said his sister had tried to kill him? He had a witness. Or what if he took the pistol from under his bed and came after her?

She trembled so violently that her teeth chattered as she walked out into the street because there was nowhere else to go and she had to go somewhere. Squinting in the brilliant light, she saw that her pink tank top was spotted with bright red blood from the scratches. Heat like fire rose up in sheets from the sidewalk, making her crazy. Tears rolled down onto the pink top, making wet blotches beside the blood, and dropped onto Pee Wee, who blinked and licked her fur.

She held Pee Wee tight, knowing the little cat was all she had in the world right now.

Leroy Patterson was running across the street toward her from the basketball court.

"What happened, Oops?" he called loudly, almost bumping into her.

"Make a hullabaloo, will ya?" she said, quickly wiping away her tears.

"You in trouble?" he asked softly.

"Don't ask nothing, Leroy."

"You in trouble. I *knew* it." He eyed the blood on her tank top suspiciously. Her knees felt like water.

"Well, get on over here while we figure this all out," he said, pulling her by the arm across the street to the court where Joelle Tompkins from Third Street was still bouncing a basketball. Opie wrenched her arm free.

"You cold, Oops?" Leroy asked. "You shaking." She moved away from him.

"You be shaking too if you just almost killed your brother."

"You tried to *kill* Frank?" Joelle walked up, her eyes bugging out of her head.

"Boy tried to strangle this cat. Think I should let him do that?" She held the kitten up for their inspection.

"Now why that nerdbrain always killing cats?" Leroy asked with that senseless sense of justice he had. It grated on her like a rasp.

"Oh, Leroy, you never understand things." It's 'cause your mama bakes chocolate chip cookies when you come home from school, she thought. And you got a father with a car who shows up regular and works steady. You the answer man, Leroy, that's why you never understand the questions we're all loaded down with.

Looking away from him she saw Solomon Leshko walking up the block toward the building, his heavy body rolling back and forth like a top waiting to fall. He had on a hat and heavy black suit coat and stopped to shift a bag of groceries, take out his huge handkerchief, and wipe his forehead. Then he poked around with his cane, loosening the dusty soil at the bottom of the little tree that grew in front of the building where he had planted some red petunias.

The three of them watched nervously as Solomon turned to go up the stoop and Frank came speeding out of the building with his baseball cap and sunglasses on. Boy didn't look any the worse for wear. Opie was amazed—and a little disappointed. Frank and Solomon stopped short and fell back as if they had bumped, then stood leering at each other. Frank leaned against the building, blocking the doorway, and lit a cigarette, never once taking his eyes off the old man. Opie hid behind Leroy, just in case, her heart pounding again.

Solomon faltered and placed his cane on the stoop. His unsteady foot groped for the step. Frank dragged on his cigarette and spewed a cloud of smoke in Solomon's direction. The old man adjusted his bag of groceries, turned his fat body sideways, and tried to slide past. Frank changed his position, blocking the door completely.

Crushing his cigarette to pulp with his heel, Frank cocked his head at Solomon and swept off the old man's hat. It was the one thing they had in common—wearing hats. Under the hat was the black beanie sitting on the back of the old man's bald head. Surprised, Frank lifted the beanie off and twirled it around his finger. Solomon made a frenzied gesture as he set his groceries on the stoop and reached for the beanie. Momentarily losing his balance, he fell backward from the second to the first step before he could grab the railing.

Opie's fists were as hard as rocks. She wanted to kill the boy all over again. Frank's foot tipped over the grocery bag. Oranges, potatoes, a chicken, and a dozen cans of cat food went bouncing down the steps, rolling out over the curb. Solomon stood there defeated, leaning on his cane, wheezing and looking as if he would collapse any minute.

Opie felt she would run screaming across the street if the torture went on a split second longer. Then Frank lost interest, dropped Solomon's beanie and hat on the stoop, elbowed him roughly out of the way, and walked his most slow, don't-care walk toward the Bowery.

"Don't mess with me, Jew man," he called ominously over his shoulder as he walked off.

Solomon put his beanie and hat back on, collected his spilled groceries from the sidewalk, and disappeared slowly into the building.

"Whew," said Leroy. "You better tell us what you wanna do next 'fore that jerk comes back again." He said it as if he thought she knew. So she clamped her chattering teeth together and decided what to do.

"First off, go catch Mr. Leshko and bring him this here cat. Say I can't keep it. Say I want to real bad, but I can't." She held Pee Wee next to her face, nuzzled her fluff, kissed her tiny pink nose, and gave her, unwillingly, to Leroy.

"Then what, Oops?"

"Well, come on back here after and I'll tell you what." He stared at her, holding the cat as if she were delicate porcelain china.

"Go on, dummy."

He ran across the street and disappeared into the building.

"What you gonna do if Frank comes 'round looking for you?" Joelle asked, nervously bouncing the ball, looking like she just wanted to go home.

"I dunno."

Opie started pacing up and down the court, as scared and empty of plans as she had ever been. Joelle leaned against the fence, watching her pace. "Hey, what's that funny-looking book you got?"

Opie had forgotten about the embroidered book. She looked down at it, touched the smooth cloth.

"Oh, sorta like a diary. I been writing in it."

"No kidding? Ain't you 'fraid your mama gonna find it?"

"My mama spend her life in bed these days," Opie said. "She lucky if she can find the bathroom." Joelle laughed uneasily and pointed admiringly at Opie's new Afro.

" 'Bout time you joined the club." Joelle had had an Afro five years. "Maybe now you gonna stop trying to be what you're not"—which meant Conk.

"Swear I'm out with that girl."

"She give you those trenches?" Joelle touched the scratches.

"Yeah. She up there making it with my dumb brother."

Joelle bounced the ball hard. "That's old news. You the only one didn't know."

"How come you didn't tell me?"

Joelle kept bouncing the ball. Opie ripped the ball away and stood facing her friend.

" 'Cause you didn't *wanna* know," Joelle said. "I seen that."

Opie looked away, the old hurt ripping her apart. Felt like life was lowering her into a deep, dark hole.

"Where's Leroy? Boy slower 'n traffic on Forty-second Street," she said, kicking the chain-link fence so hard she made a new dent.

"Leroy's cool. It's *you* who's turned down and nasty," Joelle said. She liked Leroy, bugged Opie with questions all the time about who he went around with. Kind of expected her to have a direct line on him since she lived in the same building. Opie told her his daddy said they were staying in this rent-controlled apartment to save money and move to Queens, and that Leroy had a ten-speed bike. Things like that. Joelle was a Leroy sponge. But he had never invited Joelle anywhere without Opie coming along. Made Joelle spitting mad.

Leroy finally came out of the building—but not alone! Following a few feet behind, red in the face and puffing but moving at an amazingly fast pace, was Solomon Leshko. Oh God, Opie thought desperately, leave it to Leroy and that's what you get.

Leroy hurried over to her, looking guilty.

"What you bring that old man here for?" she asked in a whisper, turning away.

"Who else gonna help us?" Us. Leroy was acting like he was in on this now, too.

Solomon leaned against the fence gulping for air. Then he waddled up to inspect her wounds and shook his head. It took a lot of head-shaking for Solomon to live on Second Street these days.

"You have done the greatest *mitzvah*—to save a life, Opal. I tell you, young lady, you are a hero." He reached out and shook her hand until she pulled it away.

Glancing back over his shoulder, Solomon rubbed his palms like a detective taking on an exciting case. "A little trouble we got here, no? But never mind," he said. "Try to kill the cat, will he? Listen."

Feeling foolish, Opie, Leroy, and Joelle leaned into Solomon Leshko's huddle, painfully aware of having no anti-Frank plan of their own. "Opal will come with me," he said. "Old Sol's apartment is one place the bum will never think to look in a thousand years, eh?" He leaned back and laughed loudly at his own cleverness and the irony of it all. The three of them glanced uneasily at one another. Solomon eyed the sun, still about two feet over the rooftops to the west, and motioned to Opie impatiently with his head.

"Quick. We haven't got much time. You can help me prepare for *Shabbes!*"

Opie didn't like the sound of it, whatever *Shabbes* was. Being locked in an apartment with Solomon Leshko, prepared or not, sounded almost as bad as being locked in a closet with Frank. But the old man had a point. Frank would never think

60

to look there. So not knowing what else to do, Opie Tyler did something that a day ago she could not have imagined herself doing. She followed Solomon Leshko across the street, up the stairs, and into his apartment. At the door she could tell Leroy wanted desperately to come in and protect her. Solomon shut the door in his face, politely but firmly.

EIGHT

Stories
from Life

SOLOMON'S PLACE SMELLED OF COOKING CHICKEN and suddenly Opie realized she hadn't eaten anything but a piece of burned toast the whole awful day. The room, with its heavy mahogany couch and wing chair, was bright with mottled afternoon light streaming through the lace curtains that hung in folds across the windows. It was true, thick hand lace, fairy-tale lace, not flimsy five-and-dime stuff.

As if in a dream, Opie moved toward the windows, forgetting everything but the creamy flying birds and twining flowers floating against the golden afternoon light. Beyond those curtains it seemed that the world might be magic—no tenements or trash-strewn parking lots.

Solomon shuffled over behind her, laying his hat on the table. "I never open those curtains," he said, reaching out to stroke them gently. "Sometimes I sit and get lost in them. Anna, you remember my wife, she's in those curtains . . . and something more I can only catch a piece of after all these years."

Opie glanced over to see if he had on the black beanie. He did. A big orange cat had jumped onto his shoulder and sat as if it belonged there.

"Would you like to hear the story of those curtains?" he asked. She nodded, as if they were caught together in the web of the same soft dream.

"Well, first sit down"—pointing to the table—"while I fix those scratches. Is the boy a werewolf that he scratched you so? Now that I would believe."

Solomon walked toward the bathroom, muttering about Frank, the cat still on his shoulder. Two cats peeked at him from the top shelf of the hall closet, another was curled in a big bowl on the counter, and yet another stared at Opie from inside a half-open drawer.

"Hey, where's Pee Wee?" she called after him.

"Who?"

"You know, Bubeleh, the cat."

"Ah, Bubeleh, that little rascal. If I know her she's sleeping on the velvet drapes right here!" He bent down, scooped her out of the bottom of the closet, and kissed her nose. Opie ran to get her while he shuffled into the bathroom to rattle around in the medicine chest.

In the hall closet was a shelf filled with silver candlesticks, some with lots of curving arms that looked like trees, and piles of silver goblets, trays, and other strange shining things. Opie closed the door tightly, feeling nervous. Maybe that silver was the "line" Frank had on Solomon.

"This shouldn't happen to a dog," he said, shaking his head and dabbing his last painful dab at the scratches on her back. As he sat down across the table from her, the cat jumped back on his shoulder and settled in. He leaned toward her. "Don't look so sad, Opal," he said. "You could tell old Sol what happened, no?" She shook her head. He put his hand over his heart. "I would never breathe one word, God strike me down and make all my teeth fall out."

Opie looked at his teeth, which looked false anyway.

"You don't believe me?" he asked. "You want a better bargain, maybe? Well, how about He makes beets to grow in my petunias, *oy!*"

"Guess I know a bargain when I see one," Opie said, smiling weakly, and bit her lip. "Chile, don't tell no one your troubles but the Lord," Grandma'am had always said. In her life Opie had swallowed down a ton of troubles she wanted to tell and they'd been laying heavy around the heart region for a few years now. But she was not gonna spill her guts to some old Jew man who called her names behind her back and said she was just like all the rest of "them."

She glanced at him. Doesn't matter *who* you tell when you're sitting plunk down the bottom of a big hole, she thought suddenly, and took a deep breath that broke open something tight stretched across her chest.

Then all the words gushed out like the flood on the Willacoochee River Grandma'am had told her about, pushing the ruins of everything before it—Frank, Conk, Ma'am even. He listened calmly, muttering quietly at places, nodding and bobbing a little sometimes like he had heard it all before. Opie felt embarrassed, unreal, as the words floated from her. The shaking came back, and the tears. He put a fresh handkerchief on the table and let her cry behind her hands. She heard him stirring and mixing in the kitchenette nearby.

She looked up feeling disturbed, like someone was watching her. It was the couple in the dark wood frame over the table. They stood in their faded world, stiffly staring, the man with a spreading beard and high-collared suit, the woman in dark dress and lace veil. Their unsmiling eyes accused her. "Intruder," they said.

"Ah, good." Solomon came up and rescued her from the wrath of his family. "I was worried I'd have to find the mop to wipe up the tears. Who would know little Opal is so full of trouble?" She blew her nose, looking away, hoping he wouldn't lay a sermon on her.

But he sat down and was quiet, his belly like a round white egg. Her eyes wandered back to the birds flying away in the lace.

"You said you'd tell me 'bout those curtains, Mr. Leshko," she reminded him.

"Ah, yes. Well now, let me see. The story begins in a little shtetl—that's a Jewish town—in Russia, where my parents lived. Life was so hard there for the Jews, they were scraping in the streets for bread. Every month a new paper posted in the town square always telling this thing, that thing, Jews couldn't do. One day the soldiers came sweeping down and boom! three people lying dead in the streets—for nothing."

Solomon looked down, stroking his beard. He had a funny habit of humming to himself when he seemed to be thinking. It almost sounded like praying.

"My father was about your age that day the soldiers came. He rushed out from the shul and there on the street he found his mother, may she rest in peace, dying with a bullet in the head."

Solomon bowed and closed his eyes. Opie glanced at the woman in the black veil in the picture over the table and saw her lying in a pool of blood. Milling people gathered around, wailing, and angry soldiers were shouting, "Break it up!"

"No!" she murmured, then stopped, embarrassed. Solomon touched her arm briefly and drew in his breath.

"After that my grandfather worried day and night that the soldiers would come again. That's why he came to America, the Golden Land." He laughed a little. "The Golden Land where they lived twelve to a flat with no heat and worked six days a week in a sweatshop sewing pants."

"But *oy*, anyway now, old Sol, he forgot the curtains. You see, back in Russia each morning people were coming in to the big market square to sell. Now a girl named Rifka lived next door to Hankele, who made the finest lace in all that region, and so she would pull Hankele's wagon to the square and sell for her.

"Later, my father worked for Rifka's father over here. They

made up a plan that my father would marry Rifka, who was still back in Russia. He said okay, why not? You see, he remembered her red hair. So he worked long hours over that sewing machine in the middle of the night to help her come to New York.

"Now I promise, I promise I'm coming to those curtains. He always told how he went to meet Rifka on Ellis Island and the ferry going back bumped into the pilings down at the Battery—boom!—and the people crowded behind the gate on that boat all fell down on the deck, but not his Rifka. She stood up tall with a new hat and in her hands was a square wicker basket, that same one you see over there.

"Later at her father's place, she opened that basket and ai yi yi, there they were—the lace curtains! And they all said, 'Rifka, where did you get such?' And she said, 'When I told Hankele the news, Hankele says, '*Oy vay,* what do I need with all this lace? Take it to the new country and good riddance!' So Rifka took those curtains and that's the way it went."

Solomon got up to fetch a little black-and-white photo in a gold frame and set it on the table before her. Two pretty, broad-faced women—one young, one old—stood outside a restaurant. The younger one was hardly more than a girl. Her dark eyes danced above the big dimples of her smile.

"That is my mother, Rifka, and my wife, Anna, on our wedding day outside of Hammer's on Fourteenth Street. So sad it's closed now—you would never eat so good. They both had the reddest hair," said Solomon, drawing back behind her to look at the picture. "So you see that's why I always plant red flowers, in their memory, may their souls always bloom."

Opie took a deep breath, remembering the last time she had seen Anna Leshko. She had white hair then and black lace-up grandmother shoes. She'd stood watching the wrecking ball swing back and forth, bringing the buildings on the block to the ground, clutching her heart as if that lead ball was thumping on her own chest. The next day the ambulance had come for her and Opie never saw her again. Solomon always said it was the tearing down of the neighborhood that killed her.

Opie looked out the window at the spot near the basketball court where Anna Leshko had stood that day. The neighborhood *had* changed. More people getting robbed and killed. More drugs. Two young winos lounged against the chain-link fence. On the cracked sidewalk at their feet scattered pieces of paper had blown against the fence like drifting snow.

"When those soldiers came 'round, sounded just like Georgia," Opie said, still staring out the window. "These men in sheets came riding into this place where my grandmother lived, dragged out her next-door neighbor, hung him to a tree in the woods. Never did know why."

"We always want they should tell us why they hate. Only God knows why," Solomon said.

Opie thought about that. "God got nothing to do with those kinda things, you ask me."

NINE

The Queen Arrives

THE CHICKEN SMELLS WERE UNBEARABLY GOOD. Opie felt her stomach cramping with a hunger that came from a year without Grandma'am's cooking—a year of burned toast, hot dogs, canned beans, and macaroni mix.

Solomon fed the cats, and as the six buried their faces in a neat row of plastic bowls on newspaper, he pointed to the hall closet.

"Listen," he said, "on the shelf you'll find a white tablecloth and lace to go over it. Pick out two candlesticks. On the next shelf in a box are the candles. Then these flowers, arrange them pretty in that vase on the table."

"You don't hafta go to no trouble for me, Mr. Leshko," Opie said, standing up and hoping he would stop being formal and just put the food on the table!

"Oh, not for you, Opal." He smiled at her like he had a fabulous secret she wasn't supposed to know. "A queen is coming at sundown."

"Queen? On Second Street? What kinda trip you laying on me?"

"Aha! You see, you didn't know we had royalty on the Lower East Side. Now get the stuff. Hurry!"

Opie frowned as she reached into the closet for the tablecloths. Marita Perez was the one with a line on Solomon

68

Leshko. She said he was a crazy *brujo*. Probably bring some head queen witch down here tonight to eat with him and make some hocus-pocus. She spread the tablecloths neatly on the oak table between the windows, running her hand over the creamy lace with flowers and stars in it. Or maybe he was just plain crazy. More likely. She took out two heavy-duty silver candlesticks, shined them for good measure, and put tall white candles in them. Well, crazy or not, one thing, he sure could cook. She could smell that. She pulled the red and orange flowers around in awkward clumps, not at all sure how they should look, and set them in the middle of the table.

Solomon was bustling back and forth, just like the Queen of England with trumpets blaring might bust in the door at any moment. He shouted directions at her. Silver! Cloth napkins! Plates! *Oy vay*, not *those* plates! Tonight, please, the white plates. The little silver tray, put it in the middle. And in the back there, get out two goblets. Ai yi yi, get that cat off the table! Here, come get this bread and put it on the tray. It was a plump, shiny braided loaf he handed her with a little lace doily on top. Who ever heard of bread so fancy it had to have a doily?

Opie ran back and forth, trying to do whatever it was he wanted. The table looked like no table she had ever seen before. Grandma'am, who had proudly possessed one unstained white tablecloth they'd used for Sunday dinners, had never been able to set a table like this. It looked like something she had seen in a magazine picture advertising the Plaza hotel. All that was missing were the potted palms—and she expected he'd bring them in any minute.

Solomon told her to hurry and clean up as he went into the bedroom. In his bathroom, little yellowed decals of seashells and sea horses were scattered on the light green walls. On a drying rack in the bathtub hung ten pairs of holy black socks and some voluminous undershorts. Embarrassed, she pulled the shower curtain shut.

Locking the bathroom door, she filled the sink with water and took off her top to scrub the blood from the front. Wouldn't want to shock the queen! Then she washed her upper body, rubbed her cheeks to bring back some color, ran the pick through her hair, and went back out, crossing her arms to cover up the wet front of her tank top.

The light in the room was turning soft and bluish. She stood in the hall watching Solomon, who had put on a new suit along with that white-fringed shawl she had seen him wear down on Second Avenue years before.

"Come, come. I want you should be here when she arrives!" he called out impatiently. Opie stood across the table, embarrassed by her cut-off jean shorts, which certainly didn't have the royal touch. She kept expecting a knock. Solomon smiled mysteriously and struck a match to light the candles, which threw a golden glow up onto his face. A sad half-chant, half-song in some language she had never heard filled the room as he moved his hands grandly over the candles like he was conducting the New York Philharmonic. Then he poured dark red wine from a cut-crystal decanter into one of the silver goblets, which he held up high and chanted over like a wizard. After taking a sip, he handed the cup to her. She shot him a look of panic.

"Go ahead, drink! Tonight we celebrate!" She wondered if this was like the bread and wine thing at her grandmother's church. She took the heavy goblet and sipped the sweet wine. He even did a little song over the bread and handed her a chunk. So where was this queen? She was missing all the weird stuff.

Not knowing if sitting was permitted, Opie kept standing while he went back to the kitchenette, but behind his back she took another big bite of the yellowish bread. It was so good

70

and sweet she stuffed the whole piece in her mouth and had to stop chewing when he came back. He set a big bowl of disgusting red soup in front of her. This man didn't just plant red, he even *ate* red for God's sake!

"Sit, *sit* already. Or maybe you want I should pull out your chair?" He waddled around, pushed her chair under her knees before she could move, then plopped in his own chair smiling broadly. "The queen, she's honored to have such a big hero at her table."

Strange things were floating around in the soup. She looked nervously at him, then at the door again.

"So, uh, she late or something?"

"Who?"

"You know, the queen."

"*Oy gevalt!* She must have slipped in when you weren't looking! She's right here." He threw his hand out toward the empty chair and loudly burst into song again.

"Come on, *sing,* Opal! She likes that you welcome her with song." He continued singing in his deep booming voice, throwing his head around like he was in some choir up on stage. She mumbled and hummed along to be polite, but her brain was darting around like a runaway rocket inside her head. Maybe he was just muttering in here to all these imaginary people—like Buddy Cevasco upstairs, who'd never really come home from the Vietnam War and spent whole days throwing paper airplanes out of his sixth-floor window. She'd *known* Solomon was crazy, Opie told herself, glad that something was like she thought it would be.

He stopped singing, took a noisy sip of soup, and shrugged. "What's to tell? The queen—she's the Sabbath. Comes in to see old Sol every Friday night without fail."

"That's all?" she asked suspiciously, bending over to sip the wine carefully so as not to spill on the lace.

"You want it should be more?"

71

"Sabbath sorta like the Lord's day? Sundays always kind of a drag for me."

"*Ach,* the Sabbath *we* have is different from yours. Like a world apart from all that out there." He pointed toward the window. "God waves a magic wand and I stop everything and take a big breath." He demonstrated by freezing and breathing to the bottom of his lungs without wheezing. "I get off the hook for a day, stop working so hard . . ." He waggled his finger solemnly. "God says, 'Sol, no cooking, no cleaning, no *kvetching,* be still already and talk to me. I'm getting lonely up here for six days by myself.' "

He raised his wild eyebrows and looked at her over another noisy sip of soup. "You don't want that good soup? That's my borscht." She looked at him blankly. "You know, *beets.* My borscht is famous!" He put the spoon down beside his empty bowl, sitting back expectantly.

She dipped into the soup and lifted the odd-colored spoonful to her mouth, swallowed, then realized she had put a second spoonful in her mouth without thinking. Not bad, she had to admit, and quickly polished it off. A strange fish hamburger that stank like the East River and had some clear jelly all over it was next. Opie figured she'd done her time with the soup and quietly filled her napkin. The cats, who sat in a ring around the table, came over and secretly ate the fish out of her hands. When she felt Pee Wee playing with her foot, she reached under and scooped her up. The little cat poked her nose over the edge of the tablecloth, then settled down into her lap.

Next came roast chicken, potatoes, peas—not even canned peas. She ate so fast that he had heaped her plate three times before she was conscious of anything but the parade of the fork up and down. Nervously laughing, she wiped some mashed potato from the side of her mouth.

"*Ess, mein kindele,*" he said, laughing with delight. "Eat, my child! Eat! Have some more chicken! You make old Sol so happy. If I had known, I would have bought a turkey this big!" he said and jumped up again to get more food.

"Oh no, Mr. Leshko. If I eat any more I might barf."

"Well then, stop already, God forbid!"

"Mr. Leshko?"

"What now?"

"She mind if we talk about what gonna happen tonight?"

He turned to their invisible guest and waved the back of his hand at her. "Go on, go on, look the other way. Let us worry just a little, huh?" Then he leaned across the table and whispered loudly. "Listen. I go around the corner to say a few prayers. You stay here, do the dishes, relax. Leave the candles burning for the queen. When I come back, a good plan we will make, eh?"

"How long you be praying for?" she asked warily.

"Oh, a couple hours."

"My mother be outa her mind if she come home, find me gone."

"Not to worry. Not to worry." He said it just as if he could protect her single-handedly from Frank and Ma'am and the whole world.

"Not to worry," he repeated. He had already put on his hat, neatly folded up his shawl into a small velvet bag, and picked up a thick black prayer book. His eyes rolled toward the ceiling as he looked back at her from the door. "Let me have a little word with a Friend of mine."

TEN

❧

Invasion

THE LACE CURTAINS FLUTTERED in the cool night breeze as blue twilight folded gently in on the room. Up over the buildings on Third Street, a white crescent moon rose in the New York sky that was always flushed with the glow of ten thousand streetlights.

Opie breathed in deeply. Finally she felt that something was breaking the back of all this heaviness. Funny how the sounds here in the front of the building were different from the sounds of the air shaft. You could hear people out on stoops playing bongos and the deep *beee-oooo* of a boat over on the river.

She cleared the table, did the dishes, then picked up a candle and wandered around, looking at each small detail of the old man's life. He was neat, that's for sure. The place looked like an antique shop with all the dark brown furniture and lace doilies. He had lots of books, and photographs on the wall.

In a narrow bedroom with New York Yankees pennants from long ago, there were photographs of a boy with curly red hair and dimples like Anna Leshko's. Opie stood for a long time in front of a colored picture of the red-haired boy in uniform. He looked very young and soft, his dark eyes longing for something.

She guessed he was Solomon's son, Maxy, who had served in the same Vietnam unit with Buddy Cevasco. Buddy had told how he and Maxy Leshko went downtown to enlist together. They were eighteen years old. Trouble was Buddy came back from Vietnam not all there and Maxy never came back at all. Buddy told over and over how he held Maxy in his arms with bullets flying over—held him until he was sure Maxy was dead. His face twitched every time he told the story.

In the bedroom at the end of the hall were two beds with white nubbly bedspreads and sleeping cats curled on the pillows. The flowered wallpaper had little bunches of purple violets tied with twining gold ribbons, which reminded her of Grandma'am's violet Sunday plates. Under the window was a bookcase filled with musty books written in that strange Jewish alphabet and on the top were crowds of red petunias.

Feeling guilty, she opened an inlaid wooden box on the dresser, which held a red-flowered brooch that she thought maybe Solomon's mother had brought over from Russia, and a gold-and-purple heart-shaped pin, probably Maxy's from dying a hero's death in the war. In the soft candlelight, the whole room had a magical feel, unlike any room she had ever been in, as if she had just stepped over a time warp into long ago.

She went back to the dining table by the windows, the cats following her like shadows, shushing their tails around her ankles, marking her as their own. She found a pen and cracked open the embroidered book on the lace tablecloth, pleased at the beauty of the two together in the candlelight. A cat jumped into her lap and curled up, purring.

This book going to be my Sabbath from now on. Other times I been writing got no particular names like Thursday and Friday. They're all called Trouble. Call down into them like big black holes. Keep walking around the rim of them trying not to fall in. But this book marks time apart to get strong. These

75

words walk me away, step by step, into the quiet,
where I can see.

She watched the wax run down the sides of the candles,
watched the sparking halo of yellows and greens around the
two flames in the dark. Sighing, she put her head down on the
open book, feeling full of good food for the first time in
months—and wine on top of it. It seemed so safe here with the
soft breeze over her shoulders and the distant hollow *bop-de-
bop-bop* of bongos.

She stared off into the dark room where shadows flickered,
thinking how funny Solomon was about his God stuff, sort of
like Grandma'am, so out front it was embarrassing. Opie had
stopped believing in God, who snatched things you wanted
away before you even knew to reach. Used to bargain with
God—like, Dear God, I swear I will not fight with Frank ever
again if you will only . . . Seemed she'd given God more and
more and He never kept up His end of the bargain anyway.

"We b'lieve, dear Jesus. Jus' stretch out your hand, Lord,
so that this chile will be saved." She could still hear
Grandma'am's deep voice rolling on into the night as she'd sat
on the side of Opie's bed. But Opie did not want to be saved.
She resisted and there had come a time when Grandma'am's
big brown hands, hands that knew how to fix or carry anything in the building, hands that had shone healing light, had
fallen dark and unlighted in her lap and she had stopped
trying.

From the moment she knew Grandma'am was dead, she had
boycotted the Almighty. No punishment Ma'am could think of
would make her spend time in church anymore. There was a
minor grief at the loss of being taken weekly by the hand to
the front pew of the Zion Church, where she had been tossed
up on high and swept down under by the roll of preaching and
singing. But the more she lived, the more she knew that God,

if He existed at all, lived far away from the Lower East Side of New York.

Her cheek on the open book in the soft candlelight, Opie fell deep into a worn-out, dreamless sleep. Next thing she remembered was a slight scraping noise. Then a *rat-tat-tat-tat.* The noise echoed through the layers of her sleep like a penny dropped down a street grate, and, not willing to wake up enough to decide if the noise was real or part of some unremembered dream, she drifted off again. Her sleep mind knew that someone was fooling with the screen on the open window, rattling it gently, pushing it up little by little. But dulled by wine and a full stomach, she let herself float.

Suddenly, she opened her eyes—wide! Some fool was breaking into Solomon Leshko's apartment! Who would break in on the front of the building? She blinked in the dim candlelight and turned toward the window, but it was hard to see anything through the curtains. Her heart pounded. Someone was on the windowsill! Silently she slid down under the table and crouched, wide-eyed, against the wall.

A flowerpot crashed to the floor beside her as a pair of legs swung in. She heard the jingle of metal and thought wildly about the orange rope with the harness and hook under Frank's bed. Conk had said it was the latest thing, breaking into apartments with mountain-climbing equipment hooked up and let down off the roof.

Her heart raced so fast it shook her body! Boots crossed the threadbare rug in the yellow circle of a flashlight, then turned toward the bedroom. She heard dresser drawers pulled out and dumped, bedclothes and mattresses ripped off, clothes pushed aside in the closet, boxes falling.

Run—*now!* she told herself, every muscle tense. But what if he came back while she was struggling to unbolt all of Solomon's crazy locks in the dark? Instead, she crawled to the kitchenette, stood up behind the curtain used to close it off, and prayed. The hall closet door opened. Oh God—not the silver stuff—Solomon loved that silver and it belonged to the Sabbath Queen! She heard metal clinking and knew that the thief was taking every piece of silver in Solomon's closet.

The path of the flashlight played slowly over the room, stopping on the two candles still burning brightly on the table. She moved the curtain an inch with her finger. Frank snuffed out the half-burned candles with his gloved finger and threw them on the table, then carelessly loaded the two beautiful candlesticks into his backpack.

The circle of light jerked over to the kitchenette. Her heart stopped. He walked over and began rummaging in the metal drawers not three feet away from her, cut his hand on a knife, and cursed Solomon as if he'd left a trap. Angrily he pulled the drawer out, then kicked it over on its side. She flattened her body against the refrigerator, not breathing or moving a muscle. Frank probably believed the old man had money stashed somewhere. As he reached to open the overhead kitchen cabinets, his arm brushed her head.

"What the . . ." She heard his sharp intake of breath. He ripped the curtain aside and shined the flashlight in her face! There was a blinding moment of complete open-mouthed stillness between them. In his eyes she saw dull unbelieving, as if the thought of his sister being in Solomon Leshko's apartment this Friday night was beyond anything he could imagine. He blinked, probably testing out whether she was a bad dream. Then, for the second time that day, he said:

"What the hell are *you* doing here?"

And for the second time she had no answer. She heard the awful snap of the switchblade down beside his leg and waited limply, like a lamb to the slaughter, knowing that a mad dash would only make him insanely angry and there was no getting out anyway. He hooked his elbow roughly around her neck, bending her over half backward. The cold steel blade nicked the side of her neck, making her skin sting and prickle as a drop of blood rolled down.

"Don't, Frank. Please," she begged in a small high voice, then thought wildly he would, now that she had surrendered to him. His hair swept her face. She spit it out of her mouth. Above her the huge shadows in his eye sockets made him look like a devil.

He tightened his grip, choking her like she had choked him that afternoon, pulling her farther down until her knees buckled and she had to fight to breathe.

"Didn' wanna hurt you," she croaked, clawing at his arm. "Jus' couldn't let you kill that cat."

"Cat? Oh, I get it. You're in tight with the Jew—thinks he's savior of the stinking world. Shit. You two gonna need some salvation yourselves, sister." The tip of his knife pressed hard against her skin, jabbing deeper just behind her throbbing jugular. Another drop of blood ran down her neck and dripped onto the floor.

"Won't tell no one—I swear! You leave me be, I leave you."

Suddenly there was a loud chopping noise down on the street. A distant and unmistakable voice called out, "*Gevalt! He's killing them!*" More thwacks, and more frenzied shouts about murder! Frank stiffened and let her drop to the floor. He grabbed his pack and rope, fled to the door, and swore over the barrage of locks the old man had installed.

Lying still, cheek on the floor where she fell, Opie listened to the commotion outside until Frank had slammed the door behind him and run upstairs. Weak and light-headed, she stumbled over in the dark to lock the door, then back to the window, where the screen was still up. Leaning out over the broken petunias, she could see Junior Joseph (the super Claude's Jamaican friend) reeling around on the sidewalk under the streetlight below. He raised the big gleaming machete knife in his hand and swung it sideways into the tree outside the front door. The knife lodged in the thin trunk. Junior struggled to pull it out and finish the job. Meanwhile Solomon came up behind him, waving his arms and swinging his cane at Junior's back, screaming, "He's killing them! He'll kill them all." Down the block, several of the little stick trees the city had planted were lying across the sidewalk, cut in half by one mighty hack of Junior's machete.

Big Mario was the first one out. He came racing through the front door like a cannonball, pushing up his sleeves, nearly knocking over old Banjo, who was sitting on the stoop enjoying the show. Joey Mudda, Claude, and Uncle Huey Chin in his pajamas were not far behind. They raced around bumping into each other like a slapstick comedy, shouting, "Who's hurt? Where? Where are they?" As they wrestled a bellowing, struggling Junior to the sidewalk, more people poured out of the building. A clutch of people ran up from Second Avenue and several cars stopped, blocking traffic. Joey wrenched the machete from Junior's hand and Big Mario sat his three hundred pounds on the wild-eyed little man until he threw up. Others wandered around, searching for the poor murder victims.

A huge crowd had gathered close around Junior and Big Mario by the time the police cars *wheeoooped* down the street and screeched to a halt, their blue lights flashing. The ambulance came next with three men and a stretcher. Everyone questioned everyone, but no one seemed to know what had happened. The police had handcuffed Junior before Solomon could elbow his way through the excited crowd to tell his story. People stopped buzzing and stared at the old man.

"Officer, that man, God forbid I should ever see such a thing, was killing those trees." Solomon's hand swept the line of injured trees along the street as the crowd obediently fell back to look. The policeman pointed at the trees.

"Mister, lemme get this straight. You want me to arrest this here man for killing trees?"

"That is what we pay you for, no?"

"I can't book no one for that."

"Well, I ask you, do you let people walk the streets with two-foot knives?" Solomon grabbed the long machete from Joey's hand and shoved it at the policeman's chest. The man fell back from the lethal gleaming blade.

"I guess you gotta point, mister," he said, signaling to his partner, who took the knife carefully from the old man. They gave each other a "watch it with this lunatic" look.

"So bring him in already and may he learn a lesson this time." Oh God, Opie thought, there Solomon went again, running on at the mouth, being so righteous that the people in the building hated his guts. You'd think a man would learn his own lesson after so many years.

The crowd began to murmur and complain about unjust treatment as the police car whizzed off, carrying a very forlorn and angry-looking Junior Joseph. People closed in menacingly around Solomon. Claude pushed the old man. Big Mario pushed Claude, warning him off.

"Damn Jew always got to rat on someone," came a voice from the crowd. A chorus of assent. Claude sensed everyone on his side for once and shook off the iron grip of Big Mario.

"You gonna *pay* for this, old man," he hissed through clenched teeth. "Try and bad-mouth us to the cops. You're no better than the rest of us, you mother." His voice dripped with the hate he'd been storing up for a year.

"I was only protecting those trees," Solomon replied calmly, with that aggravating and dangerous way he had of ignoring other people's rage.

"Yeah, well someone better protect *you* if I got anything to do about it." Claude, still smarting from past run-ins where Solomon had gotten the better of him, cocked his chin toward the building in a gesture that said he had control of things in his territory this time, not going to let the Jew slip a fast one up on him again.

"Come on. Let's go," he said, for a moment in control of the crowd, too. "Leave him to bury the dead." Claude laughed loudly as he swaggered back up the steps through the crowd and into the building. It was his moment of glory.

Finally only Big Mario and Solomon were left. They stared at each other a long moment, then Big Mario went in and Rosie's head disappeared from the window below Solomon's.

Solomon went slowly over to his tree and placed his hand over the gash in its trunk. He looked so completely alone, clutching his prayer book to his heart. His head turned one last time toward the row of ragged stumps lining the street. Then he tipped his hat to Banjo, who still sat exactly where he had been when it all began, and wearily mounted the steps.

ELEVEN

❧

The Fire of
Dignity

SILHOUETTED AGAINST THE HALL LIGHT, Solomon slowly closed
the apartment door. He stumbled over to the table, where he
sat down in the dark. One shaking hand lay on his black
prayer book as if he didn't dare to break the connection, the
other held fast to his wooden cane. He was fighting to breathe
again.

Opie lowered herself as silently as possible into the chair
across from him and folded her hands in front of her. Time
passed like scraping on a blackboard. He marked off the minutes by sighing and wheezing noisily as the cats jumped in and
out of his lap unnoticed. Whatever this pit was, Opie thought,
they both seemed to be mucking around in it together now.
She never would have believed it a day ago.

With his cane, he poked at the plant that had fallen on the
floor. Realizing what had happened, he looked sharply up at
her. She stared wide-eyed, holding her breath. His eyes fell to
where the kitchen utensils still lay all over the floor, then ca-
reened to the wide-open hall closet door. Opie twisted her finger until it hurt. Slapping the spot on the table where the silver
candlesticks had been, he demanded in his thundering voice of
God, "Opal, turn on the light. What have you done?"

As Opie obediently flicked on the light, his eyes fixed her
like a dart.

"What did you take?" Damn him saying that! He sighed. "I should have known you people are all the same."

Those words playing like a tape in his mind. Some big lesson you not picking up on, old man, she wanted to shout. Lesson can't wait or someone like Claude's gonna plunk you down in a schoolroom you not gonna like.

"Didn't take nothin', Mr. Leshko, so help me God," she said, still standing with her hand on the light switch, knowing he wouldn't believe her.

"Ai yi yi. *This* I need?" he groaned. "Don't you people care about anything?" Opie stiffened, painfully aware again of being put over there with "you" people. "Oh that I had gone to Queens when my sister-in-law asked me."

"Mr. Leshko, Frank ripped you off, not me. Came through that window." She pointed. "Cut me upside the neck, see?" She walked over, turning sideways so he could be convinced by her wound. But there was a deeper cut that he would never see.

"*Gottenyu,* Opal!" He sat there shaking his head and feeling his own fat neck nervously. "God forbid what this world is coming to! Sit down quick and tell me what happened."

She told him everything that had happened while he had been talking with his Friend—some Friend. He buried his head deeper and deeper in his hands as she talked.

"Looks like God ain't listening to either one of us," she said when she finished.

"Don't bring Him into it," Solomon replied. "Sometimes He's got a funny ear."

He plodded over to the hall closet and rooted around to prove to himself that the Sabbath Queen's things were really gone. Then he leaned his head on the empty shelf.

"You really liked that stuff, huh?" Opie said gently, not knowing what to say.

"That 'stuff' was a hundred years old. My grandfather was the finest silversmith in his town. And that brother of yours, may the devil choke him, will throw the gift of the ages away for pennies at some no-good pawnshop."

He put his hands on either side of his head. "*Oy vay,* a darkness is all over me," he moaned and started bobbing up and down, like she'd seen him do at the place on Second Avenue. Then the moaning caught in his throat and the sobbing started. It was a wail that went beyond lost silver and dipped straight down into the hurt of being a stranger on what used to be his own turf.

His crying unnerved her more than Frank's knife on her neck had. Opie threw herself into the clatter of putting the kitchen back in order and sweeping up the plant to block out the sound of his crying. She found a pile of flowerpots under the sink and transplanted the broken plant, hoping she could make it up to him for all the not-caring mean out there in the street, right here in their building. But you couldn't make a man like Solomon Leshko understand real life. He lived on another planet inside his head. Just his body was located on Second Street.

He had opened the phone book and was scanning the long columns under "New York City."

"Mr. Leshko, you ain't gonna call the cops."

"On *Shabbes* I'm not calling anyone. *You* call."

"Ain't calling no cops." She closed the phone book hard on his hand and took a deep breath. "Listen, it stinks, the shit Frank puts over on everybody, but if I turn him in, pretty soon he be back down here on the street looking for my ass. Seen people get hurt bad like that." Solomon looked at her unbelievingly, shaking his head. She added hopefully, "Maybe Frank be pawning that stuff down on Orchard Street. Where else he gonna bring Jewish stuff like that?" It pleased her to be so knowledgeable; she and Conk had often walked down Orchard to Delancey Street on Sundays when the Jewish shopping area was alive with people.

Solomon snapped upright. "A true genius you are, Opal!"

he said, blowing his nose like a car horn. "Sunday morning I'll call Abe Silver and Manny Weiskopf and we will stake out the street." He seemed almost happier at the idea of losing and recovering his things, and getting Frank in the bargain, than he might have been just having his things safe in the closet. "But if we don't catch him, *then* I call the police. Someone has to stop that boy."

Opie let it lie. Solomon walked into the torn-apart bedroom and started moaning and bobbing all over again. Opie followed him, pushed the mattress back onto the bed, and began shaking out the sheet, while two cats played under it making strange lumps. He pushed them gently out, grabbed the other side of the sheet, then stopped and rolled his eyes upward.

"I know, I know, not to worry. Sol, he's got *Shabbes* in here"—he tapped his chest—"but an old man needs to sleep, right?" It was his fair-weather Friend up there again. Opie blew out her cheeks as she smoothed the sheet. These Jews sure had weird ideas about things.

"Sorry," he said suddenly, glancing at her from across the bed after they had finished.

"Huh?"

"For thinking you would do such a thing."

Opie shrugged. "You don't trust none of us too much, do you?"

"And *you* are blaming me for *that?*" he asked.

She started putting his socks and handkerchiefs back in his drawers.

"I don' know. Guess I could understand . . . I mean, if I was on *your* side."

"Whose side are you on?" he asked.

"Can't be on your side, Mr. Leshko. You won't let me." He was piling boxes on the shelf in the closet, grunting and groaning loudly, but she had the feeling he was listening, too. "Know what? You keep on expecting bad to happen, your worst dreams might come true."

86

She shoved in the last pair of socks and closed the drawer. Leaning against the dresser, her voice shaking and angry, she said, "We all just trying to live only way we know how." Why did she feel like that day she had to give a speech in class? Maybe because of all the space between them. "Ain't easy getting pushed under by things all the time. Keep fighting to just not drown. Can't get ahead, can't make no mark, can't even dream sometimes. You just wake up in the morning and walk out the door. I don' blame these people who get all dead inside and don' care 'bout much. Been dead inside myself. Don' blame Frank neither. Boy just trying not to die inside and don' know the way."

She tried to gauge his reaction out of the corner of her eye as she started picking up the odd bits of jewelry spilled across the dresser scarf.

"Maybe you get along better if you try and understand 'bout what I'm saying." He was ready to tell her no, but something made her push on, tell this white man *her* truth. "What's coming down on this here street so big and ugly I *know* it can't be our fault. Don' care if it's bums got no home and freezing in doorways, or Jimmy Soto getting killed down there on the corner. Seems like all you ever think is blaming *us*. Even think you blame us—'cause of this." She touched the skin of her cheek.

He looked sharply up at her as he sat down heavily on the bed.

"Mr. Leshko?"

"What is it, Opal?"

"Feel like someday, I keep living long enough, I might bust outa here, you know, someplace where nothin' holds you down."

He smiled faintly for the first time since coming home. "Of that I have no doubt," he said simply. It was important to her—his lack of doubt.

He groaned as he bent over to pick the red brooch up off

the floor. With it still in the palm of his hand, he drew out an oversized handkerchief and wiped his forehead. Then his hand closed very tightly over the brooch and he stared off into nowhere.

"Used to be," he said softly, "you could walk all the way to Sixth Street and hear people speaking nothing but Yiddish." He handed her the brooch and sighed. "We knew about being poor, too, you know. Worse than you. Eight to a room and work, work, work six days a week for three dollars. But the difference was our dignity—that we never lost for a minute."

"Not poor worse than us," Opie said as she got up to put the brooch in the wooden box. " 'Least when you walked down the street pretending to be like everyone else, they never knew the difference. I can't never do that." She looked down at her fingertips.

"Hmmph," he said. "White skin, black skin, maybe it's all the same. You don't know how they hated us, everywhere we went, by the millions they killed us, made us slaves. But dignity is different. That you got to keep no matter what."

Opie closed the inlaid box thinking about dignity, wondering who she knew that had it.

"Mr. Leshko, I don' see how someone gonna be dignified when they never getting what they need," she said. She looked at him in the dresser mirror. One of the cats had jumped into his lap, and he was stroking its back absentmindedly.

"Talk about dignified," he said. "I'll tell you dignified. When your grandmother scrubbed these stairs, she scrubbed them like a queen. No matter what, she put her heart in it. *She* had dignity. You are very much like her," he said.

They sat on the beds opposite each other, buried in their separate thoughts.

"How come you stay down here, Mr. Leshko, you hate it so much?"

He sighed. "Well, there was a time when we thought to

move out to my sister-in-law's in Queens, Anna and me. But here we had memories. We had a place. People said hello, how are you? when I walked in the shop. It's not that way anymore. When Anna died, I says to myself, 'Sol, what would you do without a little *mishegoss* in your life? You walk to the store in Queens, it's so quiet and clean you get bored and fall asleep on the way home.' Here I should have that privilege!"

He burst out laughing so hard at the absurdity that the bed bounced up and down. She threw back her head and laughed with him, let go of the anger at all the traps he set for people—just for a minute. They were laughing together to scatter the bad of the day and seal in something that neither of them could quite put a finger on yet.

Opie grabbed Pee Wee in one hand as the kitten skittered out from under the bed. She picked up a little brown-and-white photograph that was lying on the floor.

Two grown-ups and a child held hands on a sunny sidewalk. On the left was thin, smiling Anna Leshko, her red hair done up under an old-fashioned hat with a little veil. She looked down at a small boy who seemed about to twist out of her grasp and run away. A dark, almost handsome young man with a fedora hat, a big drooping mustache, and a twinkle in his eyes stared at the picture taker. The three stood in front of a building with two storefronts.

"That you and Maxy?" she asked. He stared at the tiny picture as if he could jump inside.

"Maxy looks to be about three, so it was just after we moved here. *Oy,* Second Street, we thought it was so uptown. Most people we knew still lived down below Houston then."

"That not *our* building there, is it?"

"What else?" he asked, surprised that she didn't know. "What a beautiful building then. Marble and brass, big wide hallways and four-room apartments with tubs in the bathroom, not in the kitchen. I tell you, all our friends wanted to get in.

Downstairs, you can see it there, was Feinberg's Kosher Groceries, and on the other side of the door, Golden's Finest Men's Hats."

Opie stared harder at the background of the picture, trying to find something that looked familiar to her. The fancy curlicues on the iron stoop railing were the only thing that anchored her to today's reality.

"Why they block up them stores, Mr. Leshko?"

"Well, Moishe Feinberg, he stayed on as long as he could, poor man, but when they held him up with a gun he moved to his daughter's. Old Mr. Golden passed on and his sons were in California. The shop sat vacant and the window got broken and boarded up. And then we had a new landlord. It happens slowly, a neighborhood coming apart."

"Kinda sad, huh?" Opie said. "I wouldn't mind having some place to hang out and buy bubble gum at."

"Bubble gum! Moishe Feinberg had the finest penny root beer barrels and red licorice on the Lower East Side. You wouldn't even *think* about bubble gum when you went in his store! You ask Buddy Cevasco—he remembers."

Solomon got up and tucked the picture back under the frame of his dresser mirror. Then he turned and they looked at each other in the soft yellow light of that bedroom wallpapered in violets.

"Well, Opal," he said with a brave little lifting of his chin, "for this interesting conversation, I thank you. And now the time has come to bring you home."

TWELVE

A Devil on Her Back

OPIE LIFTED HER HEAD off the pillow. A stripe of watery light pushed in under the venetian blind and fell across the aquamarine wall. She squeezed her eyes together to keep a dream from floating out of her mind. In a dark room she waited in a long line of people. What were they going to see? she kept asking, but no one knew. As she moved forward, there was blue light streaming down on a white woman with a black veil who was hugging a black child, rocking, with her head thrown back and tears streaming down her cheeks. The woman had bitten her lip so hard in crying, it had bled down her chin and dripped on the child's head. That woman felt like Ma'am, even though she looked more like Solomon's mother.

Moaning softly, Opie pressed the pillow to her face. Maybe that dream had to do with Solomon's idea of dignity. She sat up and looked over at Ma'am breathing heavy, almost snoring, her lips hanging loose over her big teeth. Woman had not one shred of dignity there in bed where she spent most of her life. But in that dream she had looked like the Virgin Mary holding Jesus.

Wish she would hold me like that, Opie thought, wanting to cry. Then it came to her that maybe the child was the part of her that had died when she stopped believing the world was an

91

okay place. Same thing kind of happened to Frank, although he would never admit it. It wasn't too long after that he'd killed the cat. They had all lost their dignity, except Grandma'am, who'd just gone on in spite of everything.

She looked around at the jumble of clothes thrown everywhere in the room and the gold shag rug that looked like dirty hair needing to be washed. After being in Solomon's apartment, it all felt unbearably ugly—its disorder made her angry. She swore under her breath as she padded across the rug, taking off her nightie and throwing on her bathing suit, T-shirt, shorts, and sneakers. Screw Ma'am and Frank. Screw them all. She'd go to the beach and not care.

She opened the bedroom door an inch at a time to avoid the squeaky place. A flick of the washcloth and toothbrush in the locked bathroom and she was out, remembering to grab a towel and stuff subway tokens and money in her pocket.

Downstairs, faithful Leroy was playing by himself in the sharp morning shadows of the court. She pulled back inside the building door, but not in time—he'd been watching for her and called out loudly, walking right across the street.

"Make a racket, will you?" she said, as he came clattering in, and gave him a sour look.

"Sorry, Oops. I'm just glad ... you're okay, you know, after—everything. You spend the whole night in there with Mr. Leshko?" Leroy stared at her, and she knew he was just dying to know what kind of stuff went on in that second-floor apartment.

"Him and the queen and Frank, too," she said nonchalantly as they walked to the court.

"Huh?"

"Oh forget it. Let's play."

He stopped staring and handed over the ball.

She dribbled forward and backward, swooping in again and

again to leap and shoot. Dance, pivot, loop, leap, run, shoot, fly! *No one can catch me because I can fly!*

Leroy moved uncertainly across the court to join her. She passed the ball and let him in. They played harder than they ever had, pushed by Opie's need to wear out the sadness that was chasing her around. She pushed beyond the stitch in her side, pushed beyond the salty sweat in her eyes and mouth, running, always running, jumping higher to get on top of the sad, until all the world was a blur.

"Stop!" was all Leroy could manage, throwing himself against the chain-link fence at the side of the court as if flung out of the circle of her madness. He stood watching, gasping for breath while she ran on and on.

"Man, it's too *hot*," he called. Finally, when he had recovered, he put himself between her and the basket and knocked the ball out of her raised hands. They stood looking at each other. Her heaving breath jerked noisily in and out until the tingle of hyperventilation and an overwhelming fit of dizzy nausea collapsed her legs. Letting go of the world, she dimly felt herself sink into Leroy's arms.

When she opened her eyes, he was wildly fanning her with a pee-stained newspaper in the overgrown weeds at the back of the court. She turned away from him, trying not to throw up.

"Stay there, Oops. I—I'm just gonna run get some water," Leroy said, standing over her nervously.

"Don't go," she pleaded, reaching out desperately, needing someone, even Leroy, to be there. He took her hand and held it tight. She lay back in misery, still gulping for air, her stomach wrenching. A pain ripped through her brain, then settled in to banging somewhere near the top of her head. She opened her eyes to the bright white smoky sky fleeing above her and saw Leroy's dark face leaning over, caring. She felt his big hand over hers and let it calm her.

93

"Lemme go get water," Leroy said, and he relaxed his iron grip on her hand. He ran off into the building.

A drunk wandered into the court dragging a dirty blanket, never even giving her a glance. He spread the blanket out on the sparse grass just as if he expected friends for a picnic. Then he lay down curled up in the fetal position, his back to her. He was near enough for her to see the sore on his leg, even a bug crawling in his hair. Here they were, lying together in the vacant lot, and she knew no matter how low-down he felt, she felt worse.

The metal gate slammed and Leroy came back with a thermos of cold water and a brown bag. He fell to his knees beside her and eased his hand behind her head. She pushed him away and unwillingly sat up, leaning weakly over her drawn-up knees.

"You feeling better, Oops?"

"Feel 'bout like a piece of turd."

"Here. Take some water." He unscrewed the thermos.

She took it and dumped half of the water over her head. The cold streams running down her neck under her T-shirt and bathing suit actually revived her courage, if not her body. She tipped the thermos up and drank the rest of the water in one gulp. It shot icy little chills up and down her body. He laid before her, like an offering, a roll with jelly on it, a slab of cooked cold sausage, a chocolate chip cookie, and a can of soda.

"Never saw no one play crazy like *that*," he said. "Must be a hundred degrees out. Man, Oops, I swear you got a devil on your back these days."

"Sure seem like that, don't it?" she said, breaking the roll and taking a cautious bite. It stayed down, even felt good. Within five minutes every bit of his offering had disappeared. Wiping her mouth, she leaned back on her elbows, face toward the sky.

94

"C'mon, Oops, what kind of weird things that old man do to you?"

"Didn't do nothing to me 'cept stuff me with food so's I couldn't hardly walk. What you got in mind, Leroy?"

"Maybe it's him putting some sort of curse on you. Old buzzard hates us all."

"He don't hate us. He just thinks he does. Man just trying to live like all the rest of us."

Before Leroy could ask another question, Opie noticed Conk fiddling with the fence gate. They watched her walk casually across the court toward them, dragging her little sister Emilia by the hand. It seemed just like a hundred summer Saturday mornings, when Conk and Opie would head out to Coney Island.

Chubby little Emilia broke away from her sister, jumped into Opie's lap, nearly knocking her over, and threw dimpled arms around her neck.

Conk stood over them fooling with a lock of hair, her bright red lips pulled back over her perfect teeth in a big smile. Frowning inside, Opie tickled Emilia, who giggled wildly. Opie stared at Conk's legs, so perfectly shaped and olive-colored between her white short-shorts and her white high heels. All she could think of was Conk's hips melting into Frank's body as he swept her into his bed. Why was Conk coming over smiling like that, she asked herself, like nothing had happened?

"Hiya, Oops," Conk said lightly, as if it were Thursday and they could play the whole thing over right. Leroy stood up glowering, looking around, ready for whatever trouble was lurking, like maybe Frank creeping up on them. For once Opie was glad Leroy was so big and strong and in her corner.

"What you want?" Opie said shortly and got up herself, resting Emilia on her hip.

"Wanna hang out and go to the beach?"

"Why you asking?"

"I'm asking 'cause I want you to come to the beach." Conk put her hands on her hips. "Hey, c'mon. Let's forget this stuff. You're my best friend, you know that."

Opie felt pulled apart, strand by strand, with wanting it to be real. Nothing seemed to matter but her hunger to make it real—their being best friends again at Coney Island like last summer, lying next to each other on the blanket with music and the smell of hot dogs and suntan oil.

"Aw, you're just pulling a fast one again," Opie said, only half letting herself believe it.

"What kind of fast one you think I'm gonna pull? 'Course, we gotta bring her." Emilia bounced up and down in Opie's arms. Opie felt Leroy's foot step a warning on her toe. Conk saw it, too, and scowled.

"Get lost, lamebraino," she said with a flick of her wrist. Conk looked at Opie. Opie's eyes darted from one to the other. Then she pulled her foot out from under Leroy's and stepped, giggling, toward Conk.

"Yeah, Leroy, go bake cookies with your mother," Opie said.

"Oh, and don't forget to save us some," Conk added. Opie and Conk snickered as they went through the gate. Opie glanced back over her shoulder at Leroy standing with the ball under his arm looking after them, frowning. Something unsettling constricted her heart. Then she shrugged it off.

The train clattered and screeched its way up over the Manhattan Bridge to Brooklyn. Emilia knelt up excitedly on the seat, her nose pressed to the window, making little breath clouds. Far below, the East River, sparkling blue and dotted with boats, slipped out toward New York Harbor and the Statue of Liberty. To the right were the high gray skyscrapers of Wall Street; to the left was the low friendly skyline of Brooklyn.

"River, Emmie," Opie said, pointing. "*Río*. River. Boat—say it. *Barco*. Boat."

The child giggled. *"Río,"* she said.

"She's hopeless. She'll never learn English," Conk said, pulling her down to a sitting position.

They talked about the stupid things Conk always talked about, but Opie was glad for once not to bring up what was strung underneath their words tight enough to snap and slap them in the face. She looked sideways at Conk, trying to pick up on the excitement that always revved her up. But although the girl chattered beautifully and endlessly, like always, she seemed far away, distracted, a little too agitated and a little crazy. Opie felt rattled being near her.

"Cut my hair," she finally broke in, since Conk hadn't mentioned it.

"Yeah, I noticed." Opie felt angry that Conk never seemed to notice anything about her.

"So, whaddaya think?" she pushed, knowing she shouldn't.

Conk shrugged as if nothing mattered much about it. Opie felt her shoulders curling over and knew this time it was not because Conk made her disappear; it was because *she* wanted to disappear when she was with Conk. What did it matter whether the girl saw her or not? she asked herself. What mattered was how she saw herself.

The Brooklyn train dipped into the dark tunnel, then clattered up onto the elevated track, passing by row on row of neat brick houses all the same with hedges out front. Solomon had said he fell asleep on streets like this in Queens. She smiled.

"What you gonna do for your birthday?" Opie asked. Conk's fourteenth birthday was coming up.

Conk giggled to herself. "Oh, I dunno. Get married or

something." Opie's eyes flew open and her head zapped around. She wondered for a second if the dumb girl was pregnant, but let that thought pass on through.

"Say what?"

"Hey, forget it. Just kidding, all right? Not that I wouldn't like to get out—and *soon*."

"Don' have to give him all you got, you know," Opie said, taking a chance, knowing it was hopeless. "You get him that way, you gonna lose him that way. Seen a ton of other girls do that with him ..." Opie stopped herself from saying, "and they all end up on the garbage when he went prancing off with someone new."

"Yeah, so? Ain't nothing big. You just think so 'cause you're a virgin."

"Well, 'least no scumbag boy gonna give *me* some baby he ain't never gonna look at." Opie smiled at herself pulling out her mother's words to defend her own virginity.

"*Now* you got something against babies. *Caray!* You got something against everything. You are so chickenshit!"

"Hey, stop. Don' wanna talk 'bout babies no more, okay?"

The old lady beside Opie was starting to lean closer to catch every word of their conversation. When Opie turned to stare her down, the woman looked away with sudden self-righteous outrage.

"We gonna go down toward the roller coaster or up toward Brighton Beach?" Opie changed the subject, determined to concentrate on having a blast at the beach, seeing if they could patch things over for a day. At least Conk hadn't mentioned yesterday.

Yesterday. It seemed a hundred years ago as the train rocked on, stopping and starting, toward the ocean, which showed blue now at the ends of streets between tall apartment buildings. She wondered why she'd felt so scared of Frank last night, putting a chair up under the doorknob and all. Between

98

Neptune Avenue and the aquarium, she got it right between the eyes. The score between her and her brother was even since the break-in last night. She had something on Frank now and he would forget her trying to kill him in exchange for her silence. But what would happen tomorrow if Frank showed up at a pawnshop on Orchard Street with the silver and Solomon turned him in? Opie put that worry carefully to one side.

❧

THIRTEEN

Out of
the Trap

THE ELEVATED TRAIN SCREECHED TO A STOP at Stillwell Avenue. As the doors flung open, Opie, Conk, and Emilia stepped eagerly onto the platform and ran down the endless steps to the street below. Emilia's eyes danced as they walked along Surf Avenue with its clamor and clam bars and arcades. Opie bought her some pink cotton candy. The sky was blue here, not yellowish white, and the sun beamed in warmly from out over the ocean. It was still early. They had a good chance for a spot of sand on what would be a blanket of wall-to-wall people and beach umbrellas by the afternoon.

As they climbed the boardwalk, Emilia squealed and jumped up and down at the sight of the wide blue sparkling ocean with little waves curling onto the sandy shore. Out on the far horizon, where the water lightened to sky blue, dozens of ships steamed back and forth. Everywhere people were busy planting umbrellas and spreading blankets on the wide trash-strewn beach. Off to the south, at the end of the boardwalk, the high white trestle of the roller coaster towered against the blue sky. Opie threw back her head and breathed in the sharp, salty air. This was the place in the world where she went to feel at home.

"Ocean," she said, smiling as she knelt on the boardwalk to take off Emilia's sneakers. "Say it for Odita, Emmie. O-shun."

The child wiggled, shook her curly head, and said loudly, pointing, *"Mar."*

"O-shun." More giggles and mock exasperation.

"Mar." They were so involved in shoelaces and socks and their little game that Opie looked up in complete surprise when Conk took off at a run, nearly twisting her ankle as she caught her high heel between the boards.

Among the crowd of people on the boardwalk, Frank walked quickly toward them in sunglasses, the ocean breeze lifting his long black hair away from his face. His shiny white shirt was open to the waist, a thick gold chain across his chest.

Opie's heart sank like a stone. Conk flew toward him like a launched missile, after barely managing not to cripple herself during the takeoff. He staggered back against the cement wall and gave himself up to her hungry kiss. She twined her legs tightly around his waist.

Opie tried to move between Emilia and the developing scene, but the child crawled through her legs and they both watched with open mouths. Life seemed to be replaying the pain, wide screen, just in case she hadn't gotten it the first time. Only this time she had walked willingly into the trap.

Frank finally surfaced, parted Conk's legs and arms, and set her upright, being careful to brush his hand over her breasts. Then he looked straight at Opie, one side of his mouth twisting up in a triumphant smile. Conk's fingers traveled through the hair on his chest, but he pushed her roughly away to savor his moment of triumph over his sister.

"Hey, look," Frank said, "we're going for a little walk. See you here 'bout six." He came closer and smiled a lopsided smile with his mouth and not his eyes. "Have a blast, kid," he said as his eyes burned into hers, trying to lock her into an unspoken pact of fear.

She lifted her chin, pushing all her WILDCAT! power forward into her eyes. It spiraled up and out, smoking as it went, leaping against his face. His muscles tensed and he stepped back slightly, just half a step. But that half step told her she'd claimed her power, that miraculously over these last awful days she'd changed, that she would refuse to be deathly afraid of him ever again. And she knew that a big, sad part of him was quaking under his cool, knew it better than he knew himself. But his courage, maybe even his life, depended on hiding that part.

Turning on his heel, Frank grabbed Conk by the arm and started to pull her down the boardwalk. Opie called loudly after them.

"Hey, you forgot something!" As they turned back, she nodded her head at Emilia and smiled sweetly.

"Oh, she wouldn't dig it where we're going," Conk said. "It's too dark." She laughed a hollow laugh meant to call Opie's bluff.

"Be fascinating for her. Birds and bees. A real education." Opie picked up Emilia and walked resolutely toward them, holding fast. She felt the child sink farther and farther into her shoulder. Opie pulled her off, kicking and screaming, and thrust her at Conk. The girl stood unmoving, trusting the child to create such a scene that not taking her back would make Opie look like a child-abuser.

Emilia, whose tantrums were famous, did not disappoint her. She lay on the boardwalk screaming so loud that people a block away turned to look. She rolled and kicked and turned red and purple in the face. Then she threw herself at Opie's knees, clutching with a football hold, yelling bloody murder, *"No, Odita! No, Odita!"* Two old ladies with their beach chairs in tow stopped to cluck their disapproval and gave each other a knowing look of disgust as they descended the steps to the sand, chatting about the riffraff that came to the beach these days.

Conk and Frank began to drift away, still facing her. Opie

102

was horribly torn between her power and outrage at the trap they had set for her, and Emilia's need. She wanted desperately to shake the child off her leg and walk away into a day alone at the beach, licking her wounds and gathering strength not to be wounded again. As she unfastened a sniffling Emilia from her knees and lifted her up onto the top of the fence for a hug, she decided. She and Emilia would *both* get what they wanted, she told herself, and screw those *khazers*. She smiled at remembering Solomon's favorite word.

Opie tried to seal over the raw hurt and concentrate on letting the hot sun heal her. Emilia forgot her tantrum and started singing and digging happily at the edge of the towel. Opie leaned back and melted into the hot sand, letting her body relax for the first time in days. Here, under the sun, in the salt air, the craziness and danger and silence stopped hounding her. Here it seemed that there might be some hours of peace.

Opie got up to bury Emilia in the sand, sculpting a fancy dress with seaweed trim, laughing at her for wiggling around and cracking her sand clothes. Then they ran in and out of the cold water, splashing each other. Opie walked into the gentle surf supporting Emilia's back on the surface of the water, moving her up and over the waves. Her chubby arms and legs made furious little flutterings.

"See," said Opie, "Emmie can swim."

"*Sí—nadadora buena,*" said the child and kicked even harder. She looked extremely pleased with herself and stared adoringly up at Opie.

Emilia's lips were blue with cold as Opie dried her off. Thumb in her mouth, the child curled up next to her, right under her arm like a little bird, and they both lay back on the towel and pretended to sleep for a long time.

Suddenly Opie shuddered deep inside and for a moment felt afraid again. Opening her eyes, she stared up at the gathering clouds racing in from the sea, making her teeth chatter with cold.

"*Te amo,* Emmie," she said softly into the child's sweaty, salty hair as she brushed out the sand.

Emilia sat up and smiled as if she had a wonderful secret she was bursting to tell.

"I wuv you," she said in English. Opie hugged her tight.

They waited on the boardwalk, playing tag from six to six twenty-five by a passerby's watch. Then they got hot dogs and soda, Emilia spinning around on the stool until she couldn't stand up. When they went back to the boardwalk, there was still no sign of the dumb lovebirds. The wind had picked up and turned chilly. The golden late afternoon sun had become a watery lemon in a leaden sky. Opie looked one last time at the thinning crowds on the boardwalk and decided to leave.

By the time they rounded the corner onto Second Street, a brisk breeze was blowing scraps of paper over the sidewalk, and rolling purple clouds threatened to dump sheets of rain. Emilia slept heavily on her shoulder. In front of their building, Solomon Leshko was bending wire screening around his wounded tree. As she drew nearer, she could hear that he was having a conversation with himself.

"Let them talk," he said with a shrug. "Do they know one *tchotchke* about life? So help me, no. I build up—they tear down. Just like that—wring the neck, hack to pieces—gone, say *kaddish!* How can a man live without caring? Ai yi yi. You tell me how."

She had become immune to being part of "them" since last night and his rantings actually made her smile. He stopped for a moment, looked up at the tree, and shook his head.

"My Anna said the end was coming. She saw the place changing. 'Sol,' she says to me, 'it will never be *our* place again.' I remember her face when she told me about Plonsky's on First Avenue, that now they painted it over red and yellow and served pork hot dogs out a little window."

He continued twisting the wire until his fingers began to look as if he'd been picking up broken glass without a broom.

"Hey, Mr. Leshko, you gonna tear your hands to shreds 'fore you get done."

He started and looked over his shoulder, his face falling into a relieved smile.

"And you could do better?"

"Here—take her." He held the still sleeping Emilia awkwardly on his shoulder as if she would break, while Opie easily bent the wire strands around each other to the bottom.

"Well, this one tree be safe from all of *them,*" she said, smiling wryly and thinking, Old man, better wrap yourself up in the rest of that wire. "It gonna survive that cut?"

"Tar. You see," he explained, pointing to the gash, which was carefully painted over black, "that tar will keep it from bleeding to death. A little loving care, some talking to . . . *ach,* may it live to be a hundred and twenty."

"Mr. Leshko, why you always planting things where they not supposed to be?"

He handed Emilia back, picked up his cane, and looked at the sidewalk, thinking hard. Then he drew in his breath and said, "Because if I'm not busy making life, I start thinking about death. And that I need like a hole in the head."

"Too bad you couldn't be a farmer."

He laughed. "No, no. Old Sol, he's got his pots on the roof. It's enough." He shrugged.

Opie stood on the first step, next to Banjo, who was chuckling to himself and slapping his bony knee over something hilarious.

The first drops of rain darkened the sidewalk and smelled their delicious chalky smell. Rosie moved her piece of pink shag rug off the windowsill and pulled her head reluctantly in, but Opie could see her standing by the open window ready to soak up every word they said.

"Thanks for dinner last night. You some cook, Mr. Leshko," she said loudly so Rosie could have something juicy to talk about.

"Well, I want you should come again for *Shabbes,* you hear?" he replied, equally loudly, and winked at her. "My grandniece Arianna will stay with me for three weeks and you can meet her. Very smart girl, my niece. You'll like her."

She felt a little thrill of anticipation mixed with anxiety and amazement that he could have any relatives under the age of eighty. He signaled her to come close so that they could whisper. "The plan for tomorrow—" he said, bending close to her ear. Rosie's head popped back out as if she enjoyed sudden showers.

"—eight o'clock, knock on my door. A good breakfast at Yonah Schimmel's—then our secret mission downtown to Orchard Street, eh?"

"Right on!" She gave him the high sign and he burst into a broad gold-toothed grin in the middle of his long, unruly beard.

FOURTEEN

❧

Looking for
a Bargain

SOLOMON LOOKED ROSY PINK and ready for high adventure when she knocked on his door Sunday morning. He had combed his beard; it even looked like he'd combed his wild eyebrows.

"Good morning, Wildcat!" he said. She growled at him and looked over her shoulder at her name shouting on the wall.

"Already I'm living with it." He shrugged as he locked the door. She knew he wouldn't ask Claude to paint over it.

The morning-after-rain city sparkled cool and bright under blue skies as they walked down Second Avenue past the junk shop, past the luncheonette, past the boarded-up storefronts and the place with the star on the window.

They crossed the busy expanse of Houston Street. She stared nervously in the window of Yonah Schimmel's bakery. It was a Jewish place—who knew what weird things they served or how they would look at her being there with one of their own. At least she'd worn her best jeans and ruffled blue-and-purple plaid shirt.

Solomon loudly greeted the man at the cash register in his old language. Half hidden behind his back, she saw the place was painted shiny white and covered with mirrors and old pictures of the Lower East Side back when Second Street was uptown. It was stuffed with noisy people sitting at long tables, sort of like the school cafeteria.

In the slanted display case were rows of fat brown pastries. She was glad she at least knew a knish when she saw one, since an old man sold them on the corner of Tenth Street right next to the pretzel wagon.

They slid into chairs at one of the long white tables. Almost immediately a waiter loomed over them. His hair was parted in the middle; he looked half starved and, since he did not smile, Opie imagined that he'd just stepped out of hard times in Russia or something. Then she remembered that he was probably not smiling because this black girl was sitting at his table. His eyes flicked over her for a moment before he fixed on Solomon for their order.

Solomon gallantly threw out his hand toward her in a "ladies first" gesture. Opie helplessly tried to toss the ball back in his court. Where were the menus? Maybe they didn't *have* menus in Jewish restaurants. Not wanting to insult anyone by asking, least of all the thin-lipped waiter, she drew in her breath and cleared her throat.

"Fried eggs and bacon," she said without looking at the waiter, "and a potato knish. Large orange juice, too, please." Seemed a pretty safe bet to her. But the waiter made a noise in his throat as if he'd eaten a flaming sword and was about to spit it out again in her lap. Solomon shifted in his seat like he was sitting on a tack, and the man next to them, who had been deep in his *New York Times,* lowered his paper and stared over his reading glasses directly at her.

"Try the homemade yogurt," Solomon said quickly. "Potato knish and yogurt for both, coffee—and a Cel-Ray tonic." The waiter stomped away, throwing a distinctly unsettling glance over his shoulder in her direction.

"Mr. Leshko, what'd I *do?*" she wailed in a whisper, wishing the man beside her would go back to reading the newspaper. Solomon pulled sagely on his beard.

"*Oy,* well, pork we don't eat."

She clapped her hand over her mouth. "Oh my God, bacon's . . . ?"

"Never mind. You could know?" He patted her hand.

"There some problem about eggs, too?"

"Problem? They don't serve eggs is the problem. This is a bakery and they got two things they're famous for here, knishes and knishes."

Not daring to look up, Opie slowly shredded the napkin in her lap. Weird. All these white people eating breakfast out without eggs. He could have warned her about the bacon and not let her flounder out there with everyone in the place staring and wondering what that dumb bacon-eating black girl was doing in here.

The waiter set a glass of quivering white stuff that looked like milk Jell-O right under her nose, then kept sneaking glances triumphantly over his shoulder to savor her dismay.

"Uh. You mind telling me what's that?" she asked, after Solomon did not seem to notice anything out of the ordinary.

"Yogurt, of course. They make it here every day fresh," he said, relishing his mouthful of the stuff.

Yogurt was high on Opie's most-hated-foods list, but she lifted her spoon bravely. Funny, it was still warm, and sweet, even without any fruit in it. It was okay, and the knish didn't do too badly either. She went through the potato, kasha, and cherry-cheese knishes at the urging of a bright-eyed Solomon, and another glass of yogurt, too, before she was too embarrassed to eat any more. The man with the reading glasses had finally gone back to his paper.

At ten minutes to nine by Solomon's old-fashioned gold watch, they turned south onto Orchard Street. The narrow street, lined with tenement stores and famous for discount Sunday shopping, was just beginning to come alive. Out of the drab storefronts, shop boys and old bearded men with beanies

109

dragged tables, cardboard boxes, and racks onto the sidewalks and piled them with clothes, toys, gadgets—everything anyone could imagine buying. Shirts, dresses, and shoelaces hung on hangers suspended from metal gates and fire escapes.

Strong, rain-cleared sunlight had pushed the early morning shadows down the face of the brick tenements and flooded the street. People called back and forth, and as the crowds began to pour down the middle of the street—because there wasn't a foot of room left on the narrow sidewalks—the bustling excitement made Opie tingle.

Solomon chattered with people as they passed as if it was a gigantic party with friends he hadn't seen in a long time. Midway down the block he stopped to haggle over the price of some flea collars he wanted to buy in bulk. He and the store owner argued furiously, alternately shrugging and waving their hands and wagging their fingers at each other. Opie turned away, mortally embarrassed.

With a careless flick of his wrist, Solomon walked off rudely and went into the next shop, where he appeared absorbed in some lace handkerchiefs. The storeowner with the flea collars folded his arms and stared in the opposite direction. Assuming he was highly insulted, Opie slipped out, hoping he wouldn't notice her. Who ever went into a store and started bargaining over prices? Then the storeowner brushed past her, tapped Solomon on the back, and said, "All right already, eight seventy-five and it's a deal!" They shared a friendly handshake over the bag of flea collars.

"What'd all *that* mean?" Opie asked as they walked away.

"What's the joy of spending a dollar without a little bargain, huh?" Solomon replied with a shrug. "Never buy retail on Orchard Street," he went on as if delivering a lecture on the essence of life. "Down here the ones who don't bargain are either fools or Christians."

Opie nodded gravely, knowing she was probably both, and

110

slowed down again to match the old man's rolling gait. This must be what that Russian marketplace he'd told her about was like. Milling crowds everywhere picking excitedly over the tables. The whole scene was filled with some kind of life that definitely went beyond dollar bills and brown paper bags full of discount merchandise.

Her festive mood ended suddenly as Solomon turned away from her and began to climb a long metal staircase to a store with a torn green awning and the three gold balls of a pawnshop swinging over the door. In the cluttered window, looking as if they had been nicely arranged there by someone twenty years ago and left to gather dust, were antiques, cheap musical instruments, clocks, knickknacks, and some branched candlesticks a lot like Solomon's.

Bells tinkled loudly as he opened the door. A narrow pathway wound through the tables loaded with china, boxes, and piles of *Life* magazine into the dim recesses of the store, where one bright lamp illuminated a frumpled graying man with a fat cigar in his mouth. He was younger than Solomon, taller, and very bony, with a long, pale face that looked like melted candle wax. Opie noticed that he didn't wear a hat or beanie. He was holding a magnifying glass up to his thick glasses in order to examine a ring with a monstrous stone.

Solomon slapped his hand on the counter before the man, who still hadn't looked up, and exclaimed, "Abe Silver, how's by you!"

The man's head jerked up immediately. He squinted at Solomon through his glasses, his mouth so slack it looked like the cigar would fall out. Then he stood up, smiling from ear to ear.

"Hah! Sol Leshko, imagine that!" He came around the counter and the two men fell into a big embrace, kissing cheeks and patting backs like they were burping babies. Then Abe grabbed a tuft of Solomon's big beard and gave it a tug.

111

"You look *good,* Sol. You gonna live to be a hundred."

"Ai. You don't think the Lord has punished me enough already?"

They laughed and Abe offered his long-lost friend a cigar out of a cardboard box. Solomon put it in his pocket and said, "Nah, Abe, I got no complaints. Arthritis in the knee from going up and down the stairs all these years, but I got my friend here." He waved his wooden cane. Abe leaned back on the counter and relit his half-smoked cigar, exhaling vast white clouds of acrid smoke so thick it shriveled Opie's nose cells. Even though it was summer he had on a heavy gray sweater worn thin at the elbows.

The questions and answers rolled back and forth between them until Opie, wishing she and Solomon could get on with their secret business, started to drum her fingers impatiently on a big leather Bible sitting on a table with piles of plates. Solomon must have noticed, because he turned to her and grabbed Abe's shoulder.

"What a rudeness! Here I have a good friend and I don't even introduce, we been schmoozing so much. This is Opal Tyler from my building. We come down on very important business, I tell you. Abe, you are the one to help us out."

"You been robbed, don't tell me, Sol. They took your grandfather's silver."

"Every piece. Opal here thinks the *gonif* might come today to you or Manny, since there were menorahs and all. I want you should catch the bum red-handed and turn him in!" Solomon pounded his fist righteously on the counter beside Abe, who continued smoking his cigar and seemed pretty unexcited.

"You got to be careful," he said, flicking his ashes on the floor. "These guys who steal this stuff get downwind of a shake, Sol, they get dangerous. Hey, I'm still alive because I don't bother the police with these SOBs. Look, take it from me. Lemme pay the bum a cheap price. You pay me half. You get your silver. Hey—only for you, Sol."

112

Solomon was violently shaking his head. Abe leaned toward him, put a bony hand on his shoulder. "Sol, Sol, listen, it's easier."

Solomon looked at Opie helplessly.

"Listen, Mr. Leshko, this man is right," she said, in complete agreement with Abe Silver's non-interference course concerning Frank. "You and me can hide, let Abe buy the stuff. Then when the guy can't run out with it no more, we step up, put a warning on him, like he better not try anything on you again."

"And not turn him in?" Solomon asked. "He deserves worse—and more."

"Look," she said. "He'd be gone 'fore you could dial a phone. Hey, maybe we could get the cops to wait around with their pistols cocked all day."

"Not a bad idea." She could see letting Frank get away with anything made Solomon uneasy, like a hole had been ripped in the order of the universe. He sighed. "All right, all right. You stay with Abe here. By Manny's shop down the next block I'll wait. At five o'clock, no news, we meet here."

She went to the door to watch him ease sideways down the stairs, one by one, turn at the bottom to give her a little high sign, which she shot back with a worried smile. Satisfied, he cast off the bottom step out into the solid sea of noisy, drifting people.

She looked north over the hubbub toward Houston Street. Frank would most likely come here to Abe's first, if he came at all. She only gave it ten chances out of a hundred that the boy was going to be stupid enough to lay himself in the jaws of their trap. Probably he'd unload that silver at the pawn-shops on Canal Street and come five o'clock, she'd have to face Solomon's bobbing and moaning again and call the police.

113

FIFTEEN

✣

Dancing
with Death

IN THE DARK, TIN-CEILINGED, CIGAR-SMELLING SHOP, Abe Silver settled uneasily back onto his stool and adjusted his thick glasses. The silence between them was not a good silence. A nervous tic contorted his throat muscles every so often as he examined more old jewelry. After a long time he said, without looking up, "Needle in a haystack to catch these bums, you know. What makes you think he's gonna come all the way down here?"

"We happen to think it's an inside job," Opie said carefully, "someone local." She frowned at Abe, wishing he'd just be quiet again and let them sit in silence. She had a hundred things she wanted to think about.

"Who needs any of 'em," he continued, his mouth suddenly twisted into a sneer. "Had my way I'd shoot every two-bit crook in the city."

He beckoned her over. Pulling out a drawer under the counter that had four loaded pistols, he fixed her with an un-blinking stare, his dark eyes huge and hardly human through the thick, taped-together glasses. She shivered.

"Make this lousy city a better place, I tell you, if the pawnbrokers could get together, give 'em a run for their money," he continued, shutting the gun drawer carefully as if it contained the crown jewels. "Used to be a clean business, you know, bail out our people who maybe got themselves in a jam."

He opened another drawer to take out a half-empty bottle of Scotch and poured three inches of whiskey in a glass that had most likely been full several times already that day.

"Yep," he said, taking a big gulp, obviously relieved that he didn't have to hide his secret anymore. "Turns my stomach when I see young hoodlums come in here. But how you gonna make a living?"

He smiled a particularly sour smile that barely lifted his droopy cheeks. She remembered Frank's contempt for pawnbrokers. Frank said they were all Jewish, every last one. "Brokerman don't want our stuff, but he sure gets off on cheating us," he'd said. Now that she'd met Abe Silver, she thought maybe her brother knew what he was talking about.

She settled into an uncomfortable old armchair off to one side but in view of the counter. Mercifully, he was kept busy with customers buying and pawning the rest of the morning. She saw his system of quickly hiding his glass under the counter, rinsing his mouth with Listerine from a bottle he kept handy, and spitting into an old spittoon.

The afternoon hours brought a dull grinding dread. It ate into her like dilute acid, making her feel helpless and full of holes. The store had a moldy chill, even though it was summer. At least there were dozens of clocks bonging away the hours, so she didn't lose track of time.

At 2:35 the ring-a-ling of bells over the door said someone was finally coming in again. Abe Silver did his hurried hide, swish, and spit; then his long face fell from an oily smile into pure contempt. Her eyes sped across the store to where her brother stood by the door. Silently she squeezed back behind the chair into the shadows between a grandfather clock and a tall mahogany breakfront.

Frank had on his shiny white shirt, a black string tie, and

sunglasses; he even had his hair pulled back in a neat ponytail, which meant he was trying to impress this brokerman. But he still looked like one of Abe's hoodlums, Opie thought grimly. After glancing over his shoulder to make sure no customers were following him up the steep stairs, he walked toward the counter like he owned the place. Abe was on edge, nervously picking up and putting things down.

The two stood leering at each other over the counter. Frank shifted his heavy pack quietly so as not to jostle the silver and give himself away before he'd sized up the man in front of him. Then he leaned over the jewelry case, trying to be as friendly and normal as he knew how.

"You got some ruby earrings?" Frank asked, looking overly interested in the contents of the case. He smiled a lop-sided conspiratorial smile. "My girlfriend, you know, her birthday."

Abe folded his arms high on his chest and cocked his head toward the display case. "Jewelry's all right there." Opie could see by his tight lips and the frequency of the tic in his throat that he was trying hard not to give an inch to this hoodlum.

Frank bent to survey the case, then pointed. "That, uh, little snake pin, lemme see it."

Abe Silver didn't take his eyes off Frank for a minute while his hand groped in the case to find the pin. He laid it on the counter, but when Frank reached to pick it up, he covered it again with his fingers.

"Look, fella, you didn't come in here after no pin," he said. "I'm a busy man. What you got?"

"Hey, not so fast, mister. Lemme see that pin." They were dancing around each other, holding out in a sinister game of cat and mouse. Abe put the pin deliberately back in the case and stood there glaring, his upper lip lifting over his long yellow teeth in disgust.

"I *said* I'm a busy man," he repeated ominously.

116

"Well, hey, don't let me bother you, man. I'll just go on down the street." Frank gave Abe Silver his sassiest look, turned, and took a few casual steps toward the door.

Abe shifted forward and Opie could see he was trembling all over. "He pays lousy," he hissed. Frank looked back over his shoulder, one eyebrow arched.

"Oh, *now* you suddenly a man of leisure."

"Look, wiseass, you got something to show or you just bluffing?"

"I got silver. Good stuff. Jewish stuff. Your customers gonna love it."

Frank laid his pack on the counter and took out one of the candlesticks. Abe Silver examined it carefully all over under the light of a metal gooseneck lamp, then turned it upside down to look for a mark on the bottom. Opie watched his face, holding her breath. She saw the slight pull of his eyebrows toward the center and knew he had found what he was looking for.

"What else you got?"

Frank produced another piece, which was examined and set next to the first, rather far back on the counter. Her brother reached instinctively for his loot, but was waved away.

"I think we can make a deal here," Abe said. "You just show me everything you got and I'll give you a price for the lot." Opie frowned, noticing for the first time a slur in Abe's speech. The day's whiskey was coursing through his brain.

Once the pieces were set out on the counter, Abe took a pad and started furiously figuring, but Opie kept getting the feeling he was just biding time until something—what? He moved the pieces slowly around the counter as though it was a gigantic chess game. Frank tapped his foot, obviously anxious to get this over.

"C'mon, mister, you seen stuff like this before. How much?"

"Don't rush me, fella."

Opie's eyes widened. Abe's hand had fallen down beside his leg toward the drawer with the guns in it! His fingers groped for the drawer handle. Her heart hammered, pounded, whanged out of control as she watched the light-colored inside of the gun drawer appear inch by slow inch. Oh my God, she thought, this some horror movie or what? Seemed like everything was shifting down into slow motion somewhere in a dream and she just couldn't wake up enough to move.

Unaware of his danger, Frank tapped his foot impatiently, then looked sideways at that snake pin he wanted so much in the jewelry case. She saw a trickle of sweat roll down the side of Abe's pale face, saw the tic in his neck contract, saw a secret smile buried deep in the folds at the corner of his mouth.

"You know, fella," said Abe, completely cool, "I have one customer who'll *really* like this stuff. So here's the deal . . ."

Suddenly Opie's muscles burst wide open, like compressed springs, hurling her body over the upholstered chair in front of her. As she flew, her leg knocked the table covered with plates crashing to its side. Her outstretched arms found Frank's knees and jerked him toward the floor. Flailing wildly, he yelped in surprise and fell backward into the waterfall of breaking china, just as a deafening crack of gunfire somewhere above them knocked Opie flat on the floor.

"Run! *Run!*" she screamed hoarsely, lifting her cheek an inch or two off the dirty linoleum. Frank scrambled up, knocking against a guitar that toppled over leaving a discordant note ringing, then he fell flat again as another bullet zinged past his ear. She watched him crawl desperately on his belly, like a snake, along the narrow path between the boxes and piles.

Shouting a string of swears, Abe Silver ran around the counter waving his gun like a wild-eyed cowboy. She shoved the guitar in his path. He stepped through the thin wooden back and leaped around clumsily on one foot trying to shake it off. The gun fired again, shattering the face of the grand-father clock.

Meanwhile the doorbells had stopped ringing and she knew Frank was running through the crowd on the street, halfway to the nearest corner. It was only then, when she knew her brother was safe, that she thought about the hot pain in her shoulder. Abe Silver collapsed into a chair, his head in his hands. Then he looked up suddenly at her, and down at the gun, as if he didn't have an idea in the world what had happened. She lifted her head four inches off the broken china and lay it back down on the musty pages of the big leather Bible, which had fallen off the table along with the plates. Abe tiptoed behind the counter and put the gun quietly back in the drawer, as if maybe he could convince them both it had never happened. Then he came around to her, tripping over the broken china.

"Are you okay, miss?" he kept asking in a shrill voice as he half lifted, half dragged her onto the chair and knelt before her, wringing his hands. Opie watched the blood darkening the left side of her good blue-and-purple ruffled shirt as if it were still a dream. Her mouth felt dry and ashy, her head so light it could have taken off and floated around the ceiling. Her left arm hung down strangely as if it no longer belonged to her, so she lifted it with her right hand into her lap.

The doorbells tinkled, and she realized that Abe Silver had run outside, where he was yelling up and down the street about someone having been shot, call the ambulance. She leaned her face against the smooth blue velvet upholstery of the chair. Cool, it was very cool. Cold even, like ice. It burned her cheek the way ice burns sometimes. Funny how in the middle of cold there was burning. Maybe in the middle of burning you could find a cool place where the fire couldn't eat you up. Must be where she was now. Sort of like that quiet Sabbath place.

119

She sighed, but it hurt to breathe, so she decided to float right into the Sabbath place, to just lie back into it and let it bear her up like the ocean. She wanted to stop all this shivering and shuddering, stop all these strange people touching her body and calling out to her. Among their voices she could still pick out Abe's shrill voice as it talked to someone, probably a policeman.

"Yes, and then he just pulled out a gun. This young lady here happened to be in his way and he shot her, officer. Shot up the store, too. I swear these hoodlums are going to kill us all . . ."

"Can you give me a description?"

"Oh, certainly, certainly." As Abe proceeded to describe her brother in detail, her outrage shattered the quiet inside and she tried to rise and speak to the policeman, tell him the truth, but the people held her down, patting her like a dog, trying to calm her. Then they pushed some cloth against her shoulder and a pain shot down into her chest for the first time. Where was Solomon? She needed someone to hold on to, some piece of her own life, now, *soon,* because the little black dots were coming, crowding in at the sides of her eyes, and they were getting bigger.

"Mr. Leshko?" she said, hoping he was there somewhere in the crowd above her. Needed to tell him the truth about Abe Silver shooting that gun and stop him from turning Frank in. The woman nearest her, who kept fanning her with a Chinese fan she'd found in the store—even though Opie was shaking like she was lying at the bottom of an icy pond—bent her ear to Opie's lips.

"What'd you say, honey? You just hang on. I hear the ambulance already. Move back and give her some air. Move back and let them in. Move back, mister! Mister, the ambulance is here."

"Opal! Opal, *mein Gott,* child!"

From far away came Solomon's voice, winded and wheezing, and his warm, fleshy hand grasping hers tightly.

With everything in her she pulled him down close, close enough to hear, but her tongue was so thick she could barely talk.

"Frank didn't shoot no one." Was she really saying it or just thinking it?

"What, what? Tell me, quick!"

"Mister, you're in the way. For God's sake, move!"

Opie held on tighter. "Not Frank. Your friend, *he* shot me. Swear you won't put 'em onto Frank. Don't leave me." His hand moved softly over her clammy forehead and for just a moment she felt the Sabbath pour in again.

The dots merged as the crowd parted and a rushing of feet with new voices came at her. She felt a jostling and then a flat smoothness. But where was Solomon?

SIXTEEN

✤

The Garden Inside

THE LIGHT WAS UNBEARABLE. It worked its way up under her lids, throbbing into the folds of her brain until it burst her eyes wide open. Not three feet from her bed a bright white square of sky beamed at her through a tall window. She leaned away from the painful light, but the touch of her wounded shoulder on the bed sent her back onto her side, which was crumpled and asleep from being down on the rock-hard hospital bed so long.

A sense of multiple presences invaded her as she faded in and out of the light.

"Mr. Leshko?" she finally said weakly and heard a sharp stirring behind her, the shuffle of heavy feet, and the slight *tack, tack* of his cane on the tiles just before each step. When she opened her eyes, his bulk shielded her from the light. He bent over.

"You okay, Wildcat? You want the nurse?" A gold curtain was drawn halfway around her bed, but she could hear the soap opera that Rosie watched on the TV and figured it must be midafternoon. Long tubes dripped clear liquid into her arm from a quivering plastic container far above.

"My mother here?" she asked, unable to turn and look, but pretty sure of where the loud snores were coming from.

"Over there in the chair. We been up all night," he said quietly.

"You gotta get her outa here 'fore she starts singing. Tell her I can't take no singing this time."

"That's why she's sleeping. She's been singing all night," he said wearily. Opie cringed and knew she could never face her roommates. "Not to worry," he continued brightly. "I can handle your mother. It's *you* I got to worry about now," he said, puttering and patting her pillow with shaking head.

"You always gotta have something to worry about, Mr. Leshko." She gave him a slight smile and let him pull the covers up around her neck.

"Worry, schmorry. What is life without a little worry? The day I stop worrying you can say *kaddish,* put me in the ground."

"Hey, lucky you ran into me, huh? I gotta endless supply." She reached up to touch the thick swath of gauze and tape around her shoulder under the blue-and-white hospital johnny.

"*Oy,* I should have known. To leave you there—everything is my fault." He held his head between his hands as if he would never recover, although she was the one needing to recover. "But praise the Most High, you were a lucky girl. You got a good Jewish doctor. The bullet he got out and he told me you will be good as new, minus a little blood, in two weeks. Nothing like a good Jewish doctor." He sat on the bottom of her bed, his short legs dangling over the edge.

"Well, praise God I didn't get anyone else," she said. "Prob'ly would of killed me." She noticed a huge funeral-parlor basket of gladiolus on her bedside table. "Who sent those things? Someone think I died?"

"Don't ask. You don't want to know."

"Abe Silver, right?" Solomon nodded. It brought the whole awful scene spilling back. "Mr. Leshko, how can anyone be such a dirty liar?"

"Abe? The man is scared. Deep down inside. His father was a tyrant. Life in the city is out of control. He don't know his own place in this world no more, it's changing so fast."

"So what happened after they took me away?"

"What's to tell? The police are looking for a young man by the description of your brother who shot up Abe Silver's pawnshop and you in the bargain. But when they ask me, I don't know nothing."

She smiled up at him and touched his pink hand on the white woven blanket.

"So you see," he went on, "our plan almost worked, except that *khazer* Abe pulled a fast one. But how could we know he would shoot a gun? Always perfectly gentle, that Abe, like a lamb."

"Been storing it up for years, you ask me. And I know a lot about storing things up," Opie said.

Solomon stood and moved over close to the tall window, staring up at the white sky over the city and pulling on his beard. He didn't hum this time but shook his head in a slow, drifting sort of way, as if the shooting of that pistol had cut him loose from his anchor, from his complete sureness about the world. After a long pause he asked, "Did your brother threaten Abe?"

"Nah. You know. He was just being Frank."

Solomon looked back out the window again. She closed her eyes and said, "Mr. Leshko, should we turn Mr. Silver in?" Then she added softly, " 'Course, they'll never believe my story against his."

"Maybe your story belongs just to us," Solomon said and sighed. "Maybe Abe and Frank are both trying to get what they want, hmm? And they just don't know how."

Opie smiled at his newfound tolerance, at how he really had listened to her. Then she chewed on her lower lip and pulled at the spread. "Mr. Leshko, *you* believe my story, don't you?"

"Not a single eye blink did I doubt."

"Swear."

"Now why are you doubting me? About you I knew that night in the hall with the spray paint. I'm saying to myself, 'Here is a girl got something straight like an arrow. This girl will go far.' " He demonstrated by pulling back a bow, Robin Hood–style, and letting go a mighty arrow. "Of course," he continued, shrugging, "I say to myself, 'Maybe she got a little different idea what looks nice on the walls, but who says old men know about these things. This girl, she got what it takes.' "

Opie felt the sadness sitting on her chest, wanting to cry its way out. She wondered how anyone could believe she had what it takes.

"Think I'm gonna cry." And with that the tears shuddered up again from that lonely place in the alley with no end. She let them roll down like a river onto her neck, let him watch her sob and tremble and get runny in the nose. She was glad that he didn't try to stop her from crying like her grandmother always had.

"Get it all out," Solomon said and settled into patting her leg and starting to sniffle himself. He was a man who understood about crying—that she knew now and suddenly appreciated.

The nurse squeaked in to give Opie a pill. On the way out, she looked back over her shoulder at the old white man and the young black girl crying together and shook her head.

"Know what?" Opie said. "A few days ago my life was so plugged up, it felt just like I wasn't going nowheres. All I could ever think was wanting so bad for *something* different to happen. Then up comes all this weirdness, just blew every-thing apart—kinda like I been waiting for it somehow."

Opie looked at Solomon. "Know something else? A funny thing happened when I was laying there bleeding. Got some

125

kinda peace—like a Sabbath right down inside me—here."
She touched her heart. "You ever have that?"

"Every day I try to have it a little."

"That Sabbath you got, you know, where you stop everything and freeze? It's sorta like a symbol for this thing that
happens inside, right?"

Solomon nodded knowingly and tapped his own heart place.
"The *real* Sabbath is like a garden you plant in here. Water the
seeds and pretty soon it grows inside—just for you it grows.
Then, praise God, you got your own green place where you
can go to find the silence. With that silence, you can be strong
to face whatever." Solomon leaned over to touch her tear-
stained cheek gently. "Sometimes we got a lot to face."

She thought about the silence that had come crashing into
her life, about the garden inside, calm at the center of the
crazy whirling all around her. Loosening the tight place she
usually kept closed around her heart, she gave that garden
space to grow.

Suddenly a snort came from the other side of the bed. Her
mother stirred and started to sniffle, like she was picking up
on the crying she'd been doing just before she went to sleep.
She blew her nose and stood up, all frumpled and baggy-eyed.
Opie and Solomon looked at each other.

He got up and patted her mother's shoulder, told her that the
good Jewish doctor had said Opal would be fine. Ma'am came
bustling around, readjusted the pillows that Solomon had just
adjusted, pulled down the covers he had pulled up, and gave
Opie a kiss on the top of her fuzzy head.

"Child, don' you go to worrying now," her mother said, set-
tling in on the bed. "The good Lord been hugging His little
girl to His bosom all night long, and He not about to let go
now."

"I'm okay, Ma'am. I really feel okay." Opie tried to look
bright and energetic.

Her mother stared down at her with moist eyes, took a deep breath, threw back her head, and started to hum, getting ready to burst out in "Nearer My God to Thee." Opie looked wildly at Solomon, who quickly picked up her mother's pocketbook and pulled her off the bed, winking over his shoulder as he hustled her out, telling her they had to let the poor child rest.

SEVENTEEN

❧

The New Arrival

OPIE'S QUICK MENDING SURPRISED a whole parade of people who came to see her after she was installed on the couch at home. Overnight she had become famous. Solomon told everyone in the building about her bravery in getting back his silver and everyone wanted to view the wounded heroine. She made up stories about what had happened, but she still felt outraged to be protecting Abe Silver.

Ma'am took two weeks off and seemed happier than she'd been in years, singing hymns and puttering around the kitchen (even cleaning the fridge), vacuuming, cooking, nursing, pouring sodas, and fluffing up the pillows behind Opie on the sofa. She got up before ten and dressed fancy to receive all the curious guests. Opie had almost decided to ask her about having Pee Wee back, figuring she might be just glad enough that her daughter was alive to give in.

They watched the soaps and afterward, although their eyes stayed on the screen, they talked. Opie told her mother she longed for her father so much now she could taste it in the back of her mouth; told her about the fantasy she had that if only they could find Ellis Lee, everything in their lives would be all right again.

"Ain't never gonna happen, child," her mother said flatly.

"Why not, Ma'am? We could find him. You don't think he'd wanna see me?"

"Ellis Lee loves you, wherever he is. But hon, that man got a fam'ly by this time and a good job."

"He got a fam'ly right *here!* He got responsibilities right *here!*" Opie shouted, banging on the coffee table with her bad arm.

"You keep on like that you gon' cripple yourself for life," Ma'am said, bundling her big angry daughter into her arms. Opie lay her head on the soft cushion of Ma'am's stomach and sobbed, again. Seemed like the sadness couldn't stay down anymore now that she'd loosened her heart.

"Ma'am?" she said, looking up and wiping her nose. Her mother didn't answer right away and shifted uneasily on the plaid sofa, as if this conversation made her want to run away.

"What you want, Opal?" she said finally.

"You think my father is a good man?"

Her mother looked out the window sucking on her lip. The whir of the fan and the talk of TV commercials filled the room.

"Yeah, he a good 'nough man."

"Ma'am?" Opie sat up on one arm. "Why you think my father never comes to see me?" She searched her mother's blank face.

"Could be he don't wanna see *me*. Could be he just wanna forget 'bout being poor and live his life. He got him a good life, sugar."

"Ma'am?"

"What now?"

Opie measured the exasperation in her mother's voice, knowing she had to keep pushing. "What if you went back to school? You could get your high school diploma and learn to type. Then you could get a good job and stop scrubbing floors. You could—"

"Opal," her mother cut in sharply. "I can't hardly read. Even if I graduate college, ain't gon' bring your father back. You the one gotta get a education in this fam'ly."

129

"I could teach you to read, Ma'am! I read best of anyone in my class."

Her mother smiled at the offer and checked into the next soap. Opie shut up and lay there with her mind whirling, head still in her mother's lap.

Roiling underneath the sudden warm normal feeling of their lives was the dread about Frank. He hadn't been home since the shooting. But even worrying about Frank couldn't push away Opie's nervous excitement about the coming arrival of Arianna Litvak. Solomon had told her his grandniece would arrive the next Friday, after seeing her parents off to Europe at the airport. She'd chosen to spend time with him rather than go to summer camp this year. Opie had been to Fresh Air camp the summer she was eleven and couldn't imagine any-one choosing to spend time on the Lower East Side over camp.

She dreamed about Arianna, but her dreams were filled with looking in many rooms but finding nothing, maybe because in her waking hours it seemed so impossible to imagine what someone named Arianna could look like. And she worried constantly. She chewed her fingernails down to the quick and had to bandage one of them; she drummed on tables until her mother yelled for her to stop; she darted around aimlessly in a fog of nervous energy wondering how in God's name was she going to make friends with this rich, white Jewish girl from Queens. Why was Solomon so convinced they would like each other? Despite his stern objections, Opie swore that she would be well enough to join them Friday night for the Sabbath Queen's coming, just as they'd planned.

All day Friday she paced from one end of the apartment to the other, getting her strength back and convincing her mother to let her go to dinner at Solomon's that night. Off and on she rifled hopelessly through her closet, throwing her ugly clothes around the bedroom and threatening to take a cab down to Delancey Street to shop for new ones. Finally, she chose her jean miniskirt. It was a pitiful compromise, not at all dressy like she wanted, but at least it had some style. Deciding on a top drove her even crazier. What do you wear when you've got a two-inch-thick hunk of gauze on your shoulder and your favorite purple-and-blue shirt has blood all over it?

Finally, after much painful pulling on and off, she settled on her red tank top with a blue-and-white striped shirt over it to cover her shoulder. After a sponge bath in the sink—since showers were strictly forbidden by the doctor—she dressed and climbed up on the tub to see how she looked in the bathroom mirror. Her long, skinny legs showed too much under the short skirt. But aside from the matchstick legs, the whole picture was not bad. She decided to get Ma'am's wide white belt and pinned it way around back since it was much too big. Then she put on the dangliest earrings. A pimple on her chin had bloomed during the day, but she hadn't beat on herself this week and the old bruises were finally gone. She made a resolution to sit hard on her hands when that uncontrollable urge of wanting to hurt herself came looming up out of the alley.

Eye makeup, that's what she needed! She unzipped Ma'am's bulging plastic makeup case, put on liner, shadow, and lipstick, and leaned into the mirror rubbing her dark red lips together, trying to get familiar with the new image that stared back. Her eyes were definitely her best feature—large, black, and almond-shaped with long lashes that didn't have to be curled like Conk's.

Ma'am insisted on escorting her down to the second floor, but Opie made her go back up before she knocked. As she waited for her mother to get all the way upstairs, she heard familiar voices in the hall below. Leroy and Joelle ran up, stopping openmouthed when they saw her.

131

"Hey, you look great, Oops!" Joelle called. "Really wow!"

Opie turned away from them quickly, but caught a surprised widening in Leroy's eyes, even though he didn't say a word. She felt a sharp twinge of guilt for having told him to go bake cookies last weekend. It was one of the stupider, meaner things she'd said in her life. But she just seemed to have something pushing her lately to be mean to Leroy. And now he *would* have to come by with Joelle and throw her off center. I couldn't care less, she told herself as the two clattered on up the stairs. If Joelle was so crazy about him, let her have him. She tugged her skirt down, pulled up the crotch of her panty hose, held her breath, and knocked.

The door swung open with such force that it banged against the wall. Solomon pulled her in, careful not to touch her bandaged shoulder, and smothered her with questions about her health. Then, rubbing his hands with excitement, he led her over to the already-set table, beside which stood the mysterious, and in Opie's mind near-legendary, Arianna.

Opie clasped her hands behind her, then in front—nothing seemed right. Why did she feel so naked? She giggled stupidly and gawked while they were being introduced. It was hopeless—she'd blown it in the first minute.

Opie thought Arianna was just like her name—beautiful and exotic in her own kind of way. Thick auburn hair, which framed her face in a flurry of curls that hung to the middle of her back, big green eyes with long dark lashes, absolutely clear skin, very white—not one pimple—and tall, but not as tall as Opie. Nice breasts, too. Why did everyone else have nice breasts?

Arianna whirled around in her full, printed skirt and bare feet, landed on the couch, and beckoned eagerly for Opie to come sit beside her—all in one graceful motion. She had an excitement and loudness that was definitely like Solomon's.

Even though they were barely three feet apart on the couch,

Opie hardly heard what Arianna said. She feasted hungrily on every detail of the girl—the swing of her wrist, the flash of her teeth, the fire of her eyes, the set of her little pointed chin. She hadn't ever been right up against a white girl. Arianna's skin looked translucent and as white as the marble stairs when Queen Bess used to scrub them. Suddenly an expectant silence interrupted her thoughts and Opie, who hadn't even heard Arianna's question, said dumbly, "Huh?" Nail the lid on your coffin, dope, she thought, gritting her teeth.

"I just was asking where you go to school and what it's like," Arianna repeated, drawing her legs up under her skirt and wrapping her arms around them. She had such sweeping determined motions, as though she always knew where every part of her body would end up before she started. Opie's body parts almost never ended up where she intended, except on the basketball court.

"This year I went to this big ugly place called J.H. 25 up on Eleventh Street. You know, they got so many schools here they ran out of names. Ain't much fun up there. I mean, the teachers let the girls read romance magazines in class long as they keep quiet, that kinda stuff."

"Okay, okay now, what's your favorite subject? What's your favorite color?" Arianna put an imaginary mike up to Opie's mouth. They both laughed.

"Well, I tell you 'bout my most *un*favorite color. That's aquamarine. My grandmother made me paint my bedroom that color." Arianna and Opie wrinkled up their noses and both said into the mike at the same time, "Oh, gross!" Then they burst into rolling waves of giggles. When she could talk, Arianna said, "And now, ma'am, we were about to discuss your favorite subject."

"My favorite subject? Guess I like English, you know, writing and reading, all that good juicy stuff." Funny be discussing school. No one she knew ever talked about school, except to put it down. Solomon padded over from the kitchenette and grabbed the mike.

"This young lady, I want the audience should know, is a very famous writer. Last year she won a big prize—citywide, no less, and published in the newspaper, too!" He handed back the mike and shuffled away, leaving Opie so embarrassed that the blood rushed to her face.

"Really! What was it?" Arianna had forgotten all about the mike and looked like she was wide open to being impressed.

"Oh, they ran this essay contest and I wrote one on the legacy of Martin Luther King, Junior. Wasn't so great really."

"Gee, I'd like to read it. Can I?" Arianna got back into her announcer role and held up the mike. "Tell the folks out there—what will you do when you're a famous writer?"

"Me? Uh, guess I'll go far away from here, that's a sure thing," Opie said, grabbing the mike from Arianna.

"Now okay, the audience wants to know what *you* wanna be someday," she asked, curious about this girl who, she was sure, hadn't ever given a thought to some scumbag boy leaving *her* with any baby.

Arianna pulled her auburn hair back off her shoulders and leaned her elbow on her knee.

"I've always wanted to be a doctor. I just love biology. I even went to summer school at City College to study amoebas. Kind of weird, huh?"

Did this girl really think she'd be a lady doctor? Even though girls could say that now, they didn't really *mean* it, at least down here. But maybe it was different with Jewish girls. Opie played with the idea of being a writer, but didn't have a clue about how that happened and knew there wasn't much chance she'd find out. Down here girls did what they knew and that was mostly having babies.

Arianna took the mike. Opie's toes were permanently curled inside her white flats with the effort to be smart and correct

134

every time she opened her mouth. She pulled uncomfortably at her short skirt and wondered what it would be like to wear a swishy romantic long skirt like Arianna's—probably look stupid on a beanpole like her. Every thirty seconds or so she fought the desire to excuse herself and run upstairs, never to come down again.

"Opal. Tell me about that name," said Arianna. "I've never heard it before."

"Well, my grandmother used to say our family's rich because it's chock-full of precious jewels. We got Aunt Pearl and Aunt Ruby and my cousin, Sapphire. So when I come along, she say they just added me on to the family treasure." Arianna had put down her mike.

Solomon came over and stood before them with his hands on his hips. He was in his best suit and white shawl with all the fringe.

"Well, ladies, time to switch channels and tune in to—the Sabbath Queen!" He threw his arms out as if he were about to burst into song.

Arianna jumped up, with Opie right behind her. She had a fluid way of moving, like water flowing, sensual but not flashy like Conk's sexy swing. Opie felt hopelessly awkward and tight as they gathered around the perfectly set flower, lace, and silver table.

"Uncle Sol . . ." Arianna tapped the top of her head. "*Kippah.* Get one for Opie, too."

He went to the bedroom, shaking his head and muttering.

"Uncle Sol doesn't really think that girls should wear *yarmulkes*—you know, those little round caps," Arianna said in a low voice.

"Oh, like that little beanie he wears?"

Arianna laughed. "Yeah, like that beanie."

"I don't get why he wears it anyway."

"Oh, showing your respect for God, you know, covering

135

your head in the presence of something so big," Arianna said.

"Maybe he thinks we should be wearing veils, like her," Opie said, glancing up at Solomon's grandmother, who didn't look quite so stern this week.

"Probably. He's pretty old-fashioned."

"Man knows some stuff, though," Opie said with certainty.

Solomon came back and handed them two shiny white beanies. Arianna had so much hair that hers floated on her head, but Opie's fitted perfectly over her short Afro.

Arianna lit the tall white candles and began singing in a loud clear voice, her hands waving toward her over the flames as if she could bring the light right into her heart. Solomon's eyes said he loved this girl whom he didn't always understand. He seemed to like kids so much. Opie felt an ache in her chest for Maxy and the unfairness of his bleeding to death in some hot jungle in Vietnam.

She touched the lace curtain with the birds flying in it, trying to remember it was only a week ago that she first saw them.

They had the same meal as last week with a different soup; this time it had big round white klunkers floating in it. Opie had become so used to risking, to stepping outside of her ordinary life, that she didn't even hesitate to pick up her spoon this time. The unexpected had changed places with the expected, and she had to admit she liked it better that way.

Solomon and Opie entertained Arianna with stories of the week's endless and crazy happenings—an attempted kitten murder, a brother strangling, a break-in with mountain-climbing equipment, a pawnshop shooting. Arianna leaned forward, her eyes dancing, in turn amused, amazed, and properly outraged at Frank and Abe Silver.

"I can think of a few choice things I'd like to tell that Frank," she said with immediate indignation and a toss of her head. "Nobody has a right to hurt others that way. I don't care how angry he is inside. Who does he think he is anyway?"

Right on, thought Opie, and decided to bring the two together as soon as possible.

"Well, tomorrow my friend Conchita's having a birthday party on the roof, and who knows, Frank might show. Does the Sabbath Queen allow birthday parties on Saturday?"

"Oh, I don't do Sabbath like Uncle Sol," Arianna said quickly. "We're much less strict. It's okay, isn't it?"

Solomon put his fork down and nodded. "I say that's God's work, no? To put that bum in his place!" They all laughed together.

&❧

EIGHTEEN

Sweet Vengeance

I*T FELT LIKE* C*ONEY* I*SLAND BEACH IN* A*UGUST* when Opie and Arianna arrived at Conk's birthday party on the roof Saturday afternoon. Seemed like the whole building had been invited and then some. Most summer weekends people gathered together for a giant sun-bathing party on their private beach. Today some sat around in plastic beach chairs, while Emilia and the other children ran screaming under a spray of crystal water from a hose. In the distant haze, the pale green span of the Williamsburg Bridge loomed up like a giant's toy. Beyond it, the gray towers of Wall Street were tall ghosts in the smog, leaving only the red-brown tenements of the Lower East Side to serve as city for today.

Taped-up balloons and looped red and yellow crepe paper streamers fluttered in the lazy breeze and the silver letters F*ELIZ* C*OMPLEAÑOS*! were pinned onto the unused clothesline over some card tables with paper tablecloths, red and white plastic coolers, and bowls of chips and pretzels.

Opie and Arianna stood next to a group of sweating people in chairs, some wearing little pink-and-green paper dunce caps that Marita Perez was handing out. Big Mario had brought his new grill and was trying to fan up the charcoal and cook hamburgers. A radio blared salsa music and some of the girls from school were standing around in short-shorts, high heels, and crop tops, moving their bodies slowly in time to the music.

Rushing busily from chair to chair, Conley was talking to everyone, spreading the word about a meeting she'd had with the landlord. Said she had asked him to rewire the building, and he said no! She rifled excitedly back and forth through sheets of paper the building inspector had sent her pointing out violations the city had found in everyone's apartments. People crowded around to see the official proof that they lived in a slum.

Arianna listened eagerly to the conversation. Joelle walked up, eyeing Arianna as if she were an alien. Opie introduced them, but she could see Arianna still had an ear out for what Conley was saying.

"What's a 'rent strike'?" she asked Opie, who was glad there was something she knew that Arianna didn't.

"That's when tenants stop paying rent because things just so bad they gotta do something. So they get together and put the money in the bank instead, kinda force the landlord to fix things."

"Wow!" Arianna said. "Sounds just like the labor union strikes we studied in school."

"Least people here get some heat in winter and the holes in the wall not more than a foot across," Joelle said importantly. "Wanna see a *real* slum, come on over to my building." Opie wished Joelle would go away. Joelle was always angry at white folks. And she was sure Joelle was there with Leroy, not that she cared.

"Conley's a social worker," Opie added quickly. "I'm gonna work for her over on the Bowery."

"Work on the Bowery?" Arianna seemed interested.

"Well, she's got this recreation center going for Bowery men and she's fixing up a storefront around the corner. I get to paint and clean, stuff like that."

"Can I come, too?" Arianna was so eager she went right over to introduce herself to Conley and offer her services, which were immediately accepted.

"Well, hippity-hop. Ain't it fun slumming it this summer?" Joelle said to Opie.

"This white girl's okay," Opie said and made a space for the good feeling rising inside her. Maybe her life wasn't so colorless and inferior in Arianna's eyes. She had rent strikes and recreation centers.

"You here with Leroy?" Opie asked, to get it over with.

"Uh-huh. He and me started going 'round—well kind of."

Opie couldn't think of anything to say. Used to be Joelle was mad because Leroy Patterson never asked her anywhere without asking Opie to go along, too. But that was all changed now.

"Heard you tight with the birthday girl again," Joelle said, kind of ugly. "You like punishment or something? She don't care if you fall on a knife."

"Well, I'm over her now—for good," Opie said.

What was this feeling of dread growing in her? The scene was cozy and fun. But something was not right. Something had changed. She looked around uneasily. Over in the corner, by the cement parapet that stuck up like a castle tower, Solomon's big shiny molasses tins stood empty, messed-up brown dirt spilled down onto the roof around them. Just last weekend they had been full of half-grown sunflowers, tomato plants, and nearly blooming petunias. She stood up, feeling as if those plants had been ripped out of her own belly. Joelle stood up, too.

"What's wrong?" she asked, looking around nervously.

"Someone trashed Solomon Leshko's flowers," Opie said, pointing. She and Joelle moved over to where Conley and Arianna were still talking. Conley was praising Solomon.

"He's one of the people who really care around here," she said to Arianna. "I don't know what we'd do without him."

"Someone ripped up all of Mr. Leshko's plants," Opie broke in, pointing to the empty, knocked-over tins. The four of them

140

walked quickly over to the corner. Opie and Arianna righted one of the metal containers and tried to replant a dying petunia.

"Who'd *do* a thing like this, and why?" Conley asked. "Maybe it's vandals again."

"I doubt it," Opie told them. "Remember all that hullabaloo about the trees getting chopped down last week? Well, I heard Claude say he was gonna get Mr. Leshko. 'Course, Junior Joseph probably not bearing much love in his heart toward Mr. L. now either. Come to think of it, there's more than a few people not too hot on him around here. They just don't understand."

"Uncle Sol told me it took him five years to lug all this dirt up here," Arianna said, still trying to get the wilting plant to stand up, even borrowing the hose from the kids to soak it. "He'll be more upset about this than if someone knocked him down and took his wallet."

"You think they did it because he's Jewish?" Joelle asked.

"They did it because he keeps on caring and it makes them mad," Opie said quickly, giving Joelle a little kick.

"Wouldn't be too hard to imagine they did it because he's Jewish, too," Arianna said, frowning. "Which one is Claude?"

Claude noticed them noticing him and sauntered over, hands deep in his pockets. He stood grinning from ear to ear. "You ladies got a problem?"

"I think you know what the problem is," Conley said.

"Yeah, I *do* know what the problem is," Claude said, looking like he was on top of the world. "Might be a few *more* 'problems' 'round here before this week is done." He turned on his heel and walked away. Conley went off to corner more people.

"What's going on?" Arianna looked really worried and confused. "What kind of threat was that? I'm sure everyone likes Uncle Sol. Who could ever not like Uncle Sol?"

141

Opie and Joelle looked at each other.

"You'd be surprised," Opie said. "Claude and your uncle been at each other's throats for a year. Your uncle's not too happy with the man's idea of clean. Nearly got hisself killed 'bout it once."

Joelle giggled and pointed down at the silver tops of the U-Haul trailers in the back lot below.

" 'Member that night us kids hopped trailer tops? Don't think I ever had so much fun."

"Yeah," said Opie. "Tops got to flopping in 'n' out, vibrating up this weird noise, like thunder. Then out comes your uncle, all red in the face and shaking the fence, shouting at the top of his lungs. 'Stop! Stop!' " Opie and Joelle giggled together.

"Why did he care?" Arianna asked.

"Man's kinda joyless," Joelle said tactlessly.

"He is not joyless. He laughs all the time," said Arianna defensively.

"Think he didn't want us kids upsetting the ghosts," said Opie, looking out over the trailer tops baking in the sun. "Mr. Leshko got ghosts on that lot. We're standing on top of the trailers and he's telling us 'bout some Jewish theater that was there years ago with crystal chandeliers and all the fine Jewish ladies from Brooklyn in their furs. Limos arriving one after the other. Prob'ly thought the vibration of the trailer tops sound like applause, you know."

Joelle laughed out loud. "Limos on First Street!" she snickered unbelievingly, glancing at the boarded-up, burned-out shells of buildings waiting for the wrecking ball.

"You guys don't understand how hard it is for him," Arianna explained. "This used to be a Jewish neighborhood. Now everything he held onto is dying."

"Yeah. Now it's just full of trash," Joelle said with an angry toss of her head. Opie looked at her sharply. Arianna chose not to notice.

"God, I don't want to tell him about his plants. He'll be heartbroken," she said, looking around as she moved over to the table and took a handful of chips. "Where's Conk?"

"Oh, she's always late for everything. Takes her half a year just to put on her eye shadow." Opie was glad not to be making excuses for Conk.

Joelle laughed. "And another half year to get dressed. Kinda funny since she don't put on much."

Arianna was wearing another longish skirt, white this time, with an orange tank top, and had her hair pulled up in a way that made her look especially beautiful and sophisticated, older than her fifteen years. Around her neck she wore a little gold Jewish star on a chain. Opie could see Joelle studying every detail of this white girl out of the corner of her eye.

"Hey, hose fight alert!" Arianna announced, putting down her Coke, and ran off to join the kids. Opie and Joelle looked at each other again, then jumped in behind her to help Emilia, who had stuck her thumb in the hose opening to spray little Tommy Chin point-blank in the face. Giggling and screaming as much as the kids, the three of them turned the cold water on one another, soaking their hair and clothes and Opie's bandage and not caring a bit, they were so glad to be cool. Others joined in and it became a water free-for-all, led mostly by a wildly laughing Arianna.

Her bandage dripping, Opie backed out of the fun. It was then that she noticed her brother. He was freshly dressed in perfect white, so she knew he'd been home. Even with his sunglasses on, she could tell his gold eyes were riveted on the bold, galloping girl in orange and white with the alabaster marble skin and auburn hair. Arianna called loudly to what was now her team, leading them in an attack. Opie noticed that Leroy had become her right-hand man.

Frank looked as if he'd seen a vision. He absentmindedly took a beer out of the cooler and moved toward the water fight like a sleepwalker, forgetting to light the cigarette he'd put in his mouth. Leaning against the cornice of the building, he folded his arms, cocked his head to one side, and watched Arianna running back and forth. Her wet skirt clung to her body and so did her tank top, and this girl did not have on a bra.

Arianna suddenly left her team to Leroy and headed straight for Frank. So she had noticed him! She snapped her hair, wetting his shirt, then, being ever so cool, wrung out her skirt on his white canvas shoes. He tried to look cool himself, like this was not happening, but only managed to look surprised. Just at that moment, Conk burst on the scene, dazzling in a new royal blue minidress and heels and expecting homage from everyone, especially Frank. As people crowded around her Happy Birthdaying, Conk's eyes combed the roof over their heads for Frank. She frowned darkly when she saw him. Opie oozed uneasily over toward Frank and Arianna, who didn't know she was being pelted with poison darts, but might need to know soon.

Arianna had taken off Frank's sunglasses, removed the cigarette from his mouth, and dropped them both in his pocket, sassy as anything. With her hands on her hips she asked:

"You Frank Tyler?"

"Yeah. Hey, what am I—a legend or something?"

"Might say you've made a few waves," she said coldly.

He smiled at her, trying out his sexiest look, his eyes drifting down momentarily to her mouth, which had a tendency to pout, and then on to her breasts, which were rounding up out of her wet shirt. She crossed her arms to defend against his gaze. Frank glanced in Conk's direction without raising an eyebrow, then refocused his attention on the juicier bait. Opie moved closer still.

"You live around here, pretty girl? Maybe you and me could make a few waves together." He was walking right into it with both feet.

"I live on the second floor—with my Uncle Sol." She stepped back and waited for the effect. It took him a few seconds to process the unexpected information. As his body went stiff, she hit him again. "And I don't 'make waves' with anyone—especially not murderers and thieves. And one more thing. Lay off my uncle. Go pick on someone your own size."

"Hey baby, you got me all wrong . . ." Frank stammered, but his mouth stayed open. Conk clicked up to his side, a stupid-looking dunce cap on her head, and scowled at both of them. She knew better than to touch him and risk her mother's suspicions, but she stood edged between them. Arianna smiled sweetly at them, said, "Bye now" and "Happy Birthday," then turned and walked back to Opie, taking her arm and steering her away.

"I went too easy on him, didn't I?" she asked.

"There'll be another chance," Opie said as they walked away from the mess on the roof. "I'll come with you to tell your uncle about the garden."

Frank's eyes followed them like a magnet.

❧

NINETEEN

A Narrow Road

"So how come your brother's such a total bum?" Arianna asked, folding Opie's clean T-shirts in the Second Avenue launderette.

Opie bristled. "Ain't really a bum. Nothing down here one side or the other like that." She piled a fresh load of dry clothes on the table, feeling bad for this white girl, who was trying to understand from somewhere over there. The growl of the washing machines filled up the space between them as they folded at opposite ends of the counter.

"You woulda liked him a few years ago," Opie said. "Man, he was a funny dude. Used to be I never got done laughing at what Frank said. Boy always got some new adventure up his sleeve, too, kinda like he was the leader on our block. But the way I figure it, the leaders get squashed the hardest down here. They just want more, you know. You be wanting more, and no chance of getting even some little piece of it, turns you all inside out."

"I don't get why you're defending him like that," Arianna said. "He would've killed you. And not one scrap of a thank-you for saving his stupid stinking life."

Opie started to answer, but stopped. Arianna would never quite understand the way things worked here—just like Solomon. She loaded the piles of clothes into the metal laundry cart.

"This arm feels pretty good," she said, lifting it up gently. "Think I'm gonna go down the recreation center tomorrow. Wanna come?"

"Sure. I can't wait."

Can't wait, Opie thought with a little smile. Girl got so much energy for life she's about to jump up and bite it. They pulled the full cart out onto the sidewalk and headed south.

"Hi, Arianna," Leroy called from the court as they bumped the cart over the curb and across Second Street. "How's it going?"

"Great!" she called back and stood watching while he showed off and shot the ball easily into the hoop. "God, I couldn't do that," she said to Opie. "I'm so terrible at sports, they even kicked me off the field hockey second-string."

"Leroy's a big star on the basketball team," Opie said. I am a star, too, she added to herself and wished she had said it out loud. She went over to see how Mr. Leshko's tree was doing and touched the tarred gash, but the tree seemed greener and bushier than ever.

"I like Leroy," Arianna said. "He's cute—and smart."

"Boy can be kind of a drag when you get to know him," Opie returned. They stood on the stoop, still watching him show off. "Too perfect, you know. Got all the answers."

"Seems like he just asks the right questions to me," Arianna said, shading her eyes. "Sort of knows where he's going." Opie had never thought of Leroy that way. Asking questions. Why was it she was afraid to ask questions? Guessed if you didn't ask, you couldn't be disappointed in the answers. Her life had been so heavy lately, she hadn't even looked an inch ahead as she dragged it. But she was going somewhere, too. Even Mr. Leshko thought so. Maybe questions were the way. She decided to write a list of them in her book.

"Uh oh. Here comes trouble!" Arianna elbowed Opie, interrupting her thoughts. Frank, in his T-shirt, studded denim vest, and sunglasses, was headed up the street toward them. His eyes were fixed on Arianna, who sighed loudly as if his approach bored her completely. They watched his punky, up-and-down walk.

"Sometime I think he looks like a big bird trying to take off and never quite making it," Opie said.

"Or maybe like a little mouse climbing the sides of a bowl and sliding back down again," said Arianna, and Opie thought maybe she had something there.

He was carrying a full backpack, the same one into which he'd loaded Solomon's silver. As he put it on the ground, Opie heard a suspicious jangle. Arianna heard it, too.

"Hard at work in the store today?" Arianna asked him, meaning Frank had been shoplifting again. This white girl was pretty swift on the uptake.

"Hey man, big sale." His eyes never left her face. Opie had noticed him take off his sunglasses and put out his cigarette to please this white girl.

"You're *so* outdoorsy, Frank," Arianna said breathlessly, pouting as if she adored him, moving over so close her breasts were barely three inches away from his chest. "Backpacks, knives, mountain-climbing gear. Tell me, do you prefer your mountains made of stone or brick?"

Opie burst out laughing. Arianna didn't lose her moment.

"But my, my," she went on softly, taking his arm, "for all this mountain climbing, you're quite a sophisticated man, I hear. Do you like candlelight dinners with silver candlesticks and silver goblets? Or maybe you just eat with a switch-blade?"

Frank pulled away and folded his arms so that his muscles bulged, finally aware that he was the butt of a deadly serious joke.

"Look baby, *I* am the best," he said, jabbing at his chest with his thumb. Arianna swooned, then looked at Opie. Frank grabbed her roughly by both arms, lifting her off the ground, and set her on the first step. "Try me, rich girl. You keep bitching, you might miss out." His arm slipped around her waist. He looked as though it was all he could do to chill out and keep from kissing her right there. "I could show you life like you never seen it before."

"And never want to, I'm sure," she said tartly, yanking herself away from him. He was hooked into his punishment, Opie could see that. Frank Tyler was in love for the first time and that could be a dangerous thing.

How did this girl dare to act so sassy? Something about the order of things down here she was not picking up on. You sass someone like Frank that hard, you gonna have to pay, Opie thought with a twinge, but put it out of her mind.

"C'mon, Opie, let's go," Arianna said, fanning herself and looking straight at Frank. "It's too 'hot' out here for me." They went inside and up the stairs, where Arianna howled and laughed so hard she had to sit down on the steps to keep from peeing. Opie laughed too, but not quite so hard. She was sure Frank could hear them. When they finally calmed down, she said:

"Maybe you better cool it."

"Hey, I'm having fun," Arianna said, "and he deserves it. Let's go tell Uncle Sol. He's been so down about his roof garden getting trashed. This'll cheer him up."

As they came up to the second floor, they saw a paper tacked to Solomon's door.

"Oh my God, no!" Opie said immediately, ripping it off, the small print blurring before her eyes.

"What? What is it?" Arianna asked.

"Eviction notice. Must be what Claude meant yesterday about more problems coming. Says here he's got thirty days. 'Course you can appeal, make the landlord show cause and keep him tied up in court."

"Why would they *do* this to Uncle Sol? He's lived here fifty years."

"You know, there some pretty stupid people in this building,

149

but sometimes, I gotta say, Mr. Leshko does it to himself. Man knows how to put people over against him."

At that moment, the locks clicked and the door flew open. Opie put the notice quickly behind her back.

"Come in already, will you? Tell old Sol the latest!" cried Solomon as if they were his permanent pipeline to all the juiciest news. They marched in and sat soberly on the sofa. He served them ice cream and macaroons, his favorite cookie, which they barely touched.

Opie was sitting on top of the eviction notice as if it would erupt like a volcano. Arianna's knuckles were white.

"Are you two stinkers up to something?" He chuckled, looking curiously from one to the other.

"Oh, Uncle Sol, there was an eviction notice on your door," Arianna blurted out. Opie pulled the wrinkled paper from under her and handed it to him. He shrank away from it, as if it would cut into his chest, his face suddenly slack and gray.

"We can fight it, Mr. Leshko," Opie said, trying to sound upbeat. "I know some people who won against their landlord. We'll get Conley to help."

He didn't even pick up his reading glasses—just sat there with the paper on his knee and his hand splayed out on top of it, humming and bobbing a little. The three of them were silent for what seemed like a long time. Finally Arianna got up, sat on the arm of his chair, and put her arm around him. Opie did the same on the other side.

"Herbie's done housing cases," Arianna said gently, her cheek on the top of his head. "I'll call and tell him to come down tomorrow so we can file an appeal and win this case. It stinks, but we know who's right."

"It's the cats," Solomon said quietly. "They'll get me on the cats. A person could hit his head against the wall. I can't fight no more."

"Herbie'll be outraged if you don't let him fight this case."

"A fine lawyer, that boy. But maybe now I need a mover."

"What?" Opie and Arianna said it together and looked in panic at each other over his head.

Solomon pushed up from the chair and stood staring out at Second Street through the lace curtains.

"I been here already fifty years. Every square of that sidewalk got another story for me—who I met there, where I was going to, how I was feeling when I was going. First my footsteps were quick, back and forth, Maxy and Anna by my side, to all the fine restaurants, to the Yiddish theater, to the shul. Now that sidewalk, it's cracked and worn out, the theaters are all gone, my friends are dying, the shul is dying, every day I go slower and slower."

A cat jumped from the table onto Solomon's shoulder and curled its fluffy orange tail around him like a fur wrap. The old man ran his hand along the curtains.

"The other night I had such a dream," he said, sighing. "People were walking and their heads were down, like so, not talking to anyone else. I saw that we were all going along on a narrow road. Whenever anyone goes off that road, boom! they disappear, and so less people were walking, and less. Finally there was only one and that one was me. I tried to keep my feet on that road; it was so slanted and slick, kind of a shiny metal like I never seen. But my feet kept slipping."

He stopped, leaning his head against the cat. Opie got up, holding her breath.

"What happened then, Mr. Leshko? You get where you going?"

"Maybe we were all going nowhere, Opal. But I woke with a start, sitting up in my bed, so I never found out."

Opie stared at him. "You can't move from here. What the trees and cats gonna do without you?" she asked him, feeling a violent, painful roiling in her chest. "What we *all* gonna do without you? These people too stone blind to see, but they need you, Mr. Leshko. They need you bad. You gotta keep holding up dignity out there where they can see it."

"You could come live with us, Uncle Sol," Arianna said, taking his arm. "Dad and you could have fun arguing every day about how to grow the garden."

"No, Annike. It's Shirley I'll call," he said, as if it had been settled in his mind long ago. "She's been rattling around in that big house all alone. Invited me years ago, Shirley did."

"Not the one in Queens! What if you fall asleep on the way to the store? You *can't* go to Queens," Opie wailed. Solomon turned to her.

"You want I should stay and fight city hall? I may be crazy but that I won't do no more. Even if we win on the eviction and I give away my cats—another month, another year, there the people come again at my door, hacking down the trees, pulling up my tomatoes, killing the alley cats. Enough is enough. Finished already."

"But Mr. Leshko, *I* don't want you to go. I'll help you. I'll . . ." Opie stopped.

He turned and reached out his hand, palm up, into the space between them. She watched her own long brown hand move into his stubby pink one, watched his fingers close over hers tightly. He shook his head.

"You see? Not to worry. Friends forever, you and me, eh? You'll come to Queens and there we'll make *Shabbes* better than here, even, and Annike can come, too."

"No, it won't be the same."

"The same? Nothing ever stays the same," he said, sighing again and looking out the window through the lace birds flying. "No, I'm wrong, Opal." He tapped his heart. "Remember the Sabbath Garden we been growing in there together? That stays the same no matter how crazy it gets. You and me can be safe there, and every time you go in to take a little rest, you can remember me, too, no?"

152

Opie shook her head.

"How many windows in your bedroom, Opal?" he asked suddenly.

"What? One."

"Good. You will have one pair of fine lace curtains to dream on in the mornings."

"Oh no you don't. You *not* gonna go," she said, and she meant it.

❧

TWENTY

Stones
and Sweat

IN THE BACK OF THE BIG PEE-SMELLING RECREATION center space, one bare light bulb hung down on a wire. Conley and Carlos Rivera stood up on ladders calling back and forth in Spanish about trying to get more lights working. Piles of junk, papers, and broken furniture still littered the floor, although Opie and Arianna had carried out at least a hundred loads that day.

"Go hit that breaker switch again," Conley called to them.

Opie ran into the back room and flipped the switch to much hooting and hurraying out front. When she came back, the whole ugliness of the big dark storefront was lighted up. There were probably another hundred loads of trash lying around in the corners. Arianna, in jeans and T-shirt with grime-streaked sweat on her tired face, was sweeping papers into a pile.

"Hey, it's nearly five! You guys have been troupers," Conley said, coming over. "You won't believe this space in another two weeks. New windows, white walls, a rug. Tomorrow Carlos is bringing in a group of Bowery men who want to help."

Arianna hugged the broom as if it could comfort her. "My uncle got an eviction notice yesterday."

"Eviction notice!" Conley exclaimed. "What for?"

"He's convinced it's the cats. I mean, he does have a load of cats in there. But you can't put someone on the street for *cats,* can you?"

"It's Claude making a stink," Conley said. "If that guy'd learn how to shake a mop, he wouldn't have time for all this mischief. Look, I can help, I'm sure. He should file an appeal immediately. Bring him down to the office first thing in the morning."

"It's worse than that," Opie told her. "What I mean is, Mr. Leshko's given up. Don't even wanna fight it. Says he gonna move out to Queens."

"Oh no." Conley stood with a box full of old papers in her arms. "What a loss that would be to the neighborhood," she said slowly, starting toward the door. Opie and Arianna loaded up and followed her to the big green dumpster on the street. The Bowery men waiting in the shade of a ripped-up awning to get into the mission soup kitchen next door eyed them with curiosity.

"I know he feels like a stranger in a strange land with the neighborhood changing so much," Conley said, watching three winos wipe windshields with dry handkerchiefs and hold out their hands to the drivers, who mostly rolled up their windows and looked the other way.

The three of them walked over toward the vacant lot on the corner. "But there's a real place for him. You know, this neighborhood is so great because it's woven together with all these bright-colored strands," she said as they went into the lot. "The colors together make the fabric beautiful. And Mr. Leshko's right in the middle of the fabric. Pull out that thread and the whole piece gets duller."

"That was beautiful," Arianna said. "Like poetry."

"It's not poetry. It's reality," Conley told her. "How do you think we could convince him to stay?"

Each buried in her own whirling thoughts, they walked

across the narrow trash-strewn lot that stretched along Houston Street. A charred barrel, which held a roaring fire in the winter where men crowded around to keep warm, stood empty in the middle of the lot. Against a wall of the recreation center building someone had built a little cardboard-and-scrap-wood shanty. Thin olive grass and some scattered purple and white wildflowers grew in scattered patches on the rocky, broken-brick surface.

"How *can* we change his mind?" Arianna was saying as they walked. Opie's eyes followed the zigzagging path of a yellow butterfly as it lit on one of the flowers, folded and flexed its wings, then flew off through the grass. She kicked at the dry, hard-packed soil, then pulled up a clump of grass and stared at the roots. Kneeling, she dragged her hand along the surface of the soil, dug into it, pushing aside rubble and rocks, sifting the coarse grains through her fingers.

"Who owns this lot?" she called after Conley.

"The city. This'll all be new buildings someday. But don't hold your breath. The city's broke. Why?"

"I have an idea," Opie said. Something seemed to be speaking through her, because even then she was not quite sure what she would say. Conley and Arianna walked eagerly back toward her. She held up a handful of dry gray soil.

"We could make a garden—right here."

"A garden? That's a nice idea, but it won't solve anything," Arianna said, looking down at her impatiently.

"Don't be so sure," Opie replied. Conley knelt down beside her to listen. "May take some time to turn that stubborn old man 'round. But if we start it, he'll finish it with us, I just know. Told me once he wanted to be a farmer. Give the man a chance to live his dreams right here on his own block. How he gonna say no?"

"But this place is a dump," Arianna said, looking around. "We'd have to work years to get anything to grow here."

156

"I ain't afraid of work, are you?" Opie said, even then afraid of what she said. "What other chance we got? Mr. Leshko's *gotta* stay. He'd be miserable in Queens."

Arianna put her hand on Opie's shoulder. "You really love him, don't you?" she said.

Opie looked down and pulled up another clump of grass. "Guess I kinda do."

She could see that Conley was already turning her idea around, mixing it with wild visions that were way beyond Solomon Leshko's being a farmer. "A community garden," she said as if in a dream. "What a great idea! We could get all the neighborhood people together with the Bowery men and clean up this soil, plant trees, flowers, vegetables, compost even. The city's planning to fence it in anyway. I'll just get them to put a gate in the fence. Opie Tyler, you're a genius! I'm sure I can get permission tomorrow. But what about money? We'll need some money fast. And a meeting."

"What if Uncle Sol moves away?" Arianna asked, still unconvinced.

"Just think positive," Opie said. "If we work hard enough, how he gonna resist?"

That very afternoon, Solomon went down to the kosher deli on Houston Street with his laundry cart to pick up a load of boxes. He piled them up in the corner of his living room, empty but ready, as if to assure himself this was really happening. He talked on the phone to his sister-in-law, Shirley, in Queens, making arrangements for everything and plans to go out to see her the next day. It was settled that Opie would somehow convince her mother to live with Pee Wee; that Arianna would take two cats home, her parents willing; and Solomon would keep three. Herbie, Shirley's grandson, upset at not being able to save his greatuncle through the law, agreed to load and drive the U-Haul when the time came. And

Solomon had already begun to think about auctioning off his furniture.

He made his moves carefully, but he dragged out his actions. People in the building heard right away, because Claude had told Rosie and Rosie had called up to Solomon from her window and he told her his plans. They began to treat him as if he were already gone, except Millie Cevasco, Buddy's mother, and Uncle Huey Chin, who'd lived there the longest and would miss him the most. Claude had a big smile on his face, knowing that the battle had been won so easily. Frank gloated, too, but privately, since he was still hotly chasing Arianna, who continued to snub him mercilessly.

Opie threw herself into the garden as if it were a championship basketball game. That first night she lay on her bed reading, underlining, and rereading all the booklets Conley had dug out of her files on reclaiming city soil and making things grow in urban environments. But the garden didn't seem any nearer to her than it had before. She sighed, turned off the light, and lay back, staring up into the hot half-dark. What if Solomon didn't come around? Somehow we'll do it anyway, she told herself bravely, not quite believing it. Leroy and Joelle had jumped in right behind her when they heard the idea. "Kids can do this," she said out loud. "Don't know how, but we can."

As the first pale light seeped in around the venetian blind the next morning, she bolted out of bed and raced down to the lot early enough to see the sun rise over the east end of Houston Street. The dawn delivery trucks were already roaring across town through the golden coolness. Dewdrops glistened on the hardscrabble grass.

She kicked along the scarred surface, not feeling half as bold as the previous night, thinking, Whatever made me believe we could turn a dump into a garden? Why not just hang out this summer, take it easy—play a little ball, read a few books, go to Coney Island? What do I care about some old white man moving out to Queens? Makes no sense at all. But that old man believes in me. That old man says I got dignity deep down. And now he's gonna go. They all go like that. Ellis Lee. Grandma'am.

"No!" She stamped her foot. This garden had to do with roots and staying and making all their lives better. This garden had to do with all their dignity. And the time for dignity had come. They could pull it off. First, they had to clean out the trash, weeds, bricks, and glass—and all that took was serious elbow grease, as Grandma'am would have said.

Conley made a bunch of phone calls to get permission and a couple of hundred-dollar donations from some community organizations. Opie, Leroy, Joelle, and Arianna rode the subway out to a nursery in Brooklyn to buy two big wheelbarrow-type carts, shovels, rakes, and gloves. It was really fun. They walked up and down the rows of trees and flowers, memorizing names they had never heard before, saying this one or that one they *had* to have in the garden, their dreams growing bigger and crazier by the minute. The huge garden carts made people on the subway look at them like they were from outer space. They just giggled. Opie thought, This is the way it should be; this is what it used to be like when all us kids thought about was having fun and being friends and no one was trying to be better than anyone else.

When they got back, Conley said she'd opened a bank account under the name Community Garden. That afternoon she ran off flyers calling people to a meeting Sunday afternoon in the garden. Opie and Arianna put them up and handed them out all over the neighborhood. They gave one to Solomon, who grunted and looked up at the girls as if they were being "stinkers" again, then went back to cleaning out his closet.

Carlos Rivera, who was supervising the Bowery men in the recreation center, brought down a few members of the Fourth

Street Social Club the next day to help out. They formed an assembly line, making pyramidlike mounds of rock and debris all over the lot, which the cart people loaded and the dumpster people unloaded. Once they had raked off the surface and pulled up all the weeds, they turned the packed soil over with shovels, broke it up, and started again.

Arianna got the idea of saving bricks in a pile to line the pathways and use as garden edgers, and since there had once been buildings in the lot, the pile grew quickly. Leroy found some heavy wire screening and rigged up a sifter with a wood frame that separated out the glass, pebbles, cement, and old dog poop.

People coming up the corner subway stairs gathered on the sidewalk to stare as if a fifty-story building were going up. Rosie Phillipo came down and stood around looking with her arms folded so that she could report on their progress to all the people in their building. Dominic and Joey from the building came back from the fish market in the early afternoon and cheerfully carried a few loads, even though they were tired. Father Basil from St. Stanislaus Church was amazed and handed them a five-dollar bill. He promised to send over members of the church youth club.

The second afternoon, Opie was jumping with both feet on a shovel to break through the iron ground, when she heard a familiar voice behind her.

"Missy." It was Banjo.

"What you want, old man?" she asked, smiling up at him. "You come to help?"

"I'se here to ask 'bout my house," he said, pointing to the patched-together shanty over by the wall. It had an old blue-and-white plastic tablecloth on top of it and a stained mattress stuffed inside. By the door stood a three-legged kitchen chair.

"Nice house," Opie said.

"Yes'm, sure is. You know old Banjo don't like that hotel.

160

Wardens always breathing down a man's neck." And throwing his bottles away, thought Opie, noticing the top of a wine bottle in his pocket.

Opie patted his shoulder. "We got no plans to tear it down, Pops, if that's what you mean," she said. "How 'bout you be the night watchman?" He burst out in a toothless grin.

"Now that's right kind of you, missy." He kicked the dirt with his old untied shoes that were all turned over to one side. "What you gon' do here to my yard?"

"Done picked the right neighborhood this time, Banjo. Your yard gonna be real uptown when we finish it. We planting a garden."

"You don't say. Gon' put a garden right here by my front door? Well, how 'bout that." Banjo kept hovering while she dug.

"What we gon' do 'bout the barrel of fire?" he asked finally. She and Leroy had moved the charred barrel over beside the shanty last week.

"That barrel like my lady come winter," he said. "She the only one ever keeps me warm." Opie remembered the men crowded around the roaring flames on cold nights, how they scoured the neighborhood for scrap wood and boxes. That barrel kept them from freezing to death in doorways. "Us men can't do without her, but the police, you know, they say we can't put her on the street. Only place they don't bother with us is this here lot."

"How 'bout we make a place of honor for that barrel, right over there in the middle? Wintertimes the garden is yours. But no peeing."

"All the men thanks you. You a good little girl, missy." He smiled down at her, his hair like crinkly cotton around his face, and she thought he would've made a great grandfather, if the bottle hadn't got him first.

He picked up one stone off the top of the nearest pile and

161

wove off toward the dumpster, getting totally distracted on the way. Opie watched him for a minute. Man had a world all his own. After another trip or two, he sat down in the three-legged chair against the wall of his house, shouting out friendly encouragement and orders between swigs of wine.

They sweated a bucketful of sweat that day. It rained Saturday, but Opie pushed them all to work anyway, saying that everything good had to start small and hard and muddy like this. They didn't have much time, she said, meaning time to win over Solomon Leshko. The Sunday meeting turned out only seven people, who stood under their umbrellas in the mud and rain and tried to look interested. But they signed on three more people, who agreed to show up the next day and help.

TWENTY-ONE

TWENTY-ONE

Footprints in the Dirt

MONDAY MORNING, OPIE RACED OUT EARLY AGAIN. City workers were busy putting up the fence. The cement truck whirled, hammers rang out, metal poles sprouted all around the lot, waiting for the huge rolls of chain link. The idea of a fence was comforting; it would seal off their little magic place. They'd plant morning glories to grow on the fence right away, she thought, just like the ones Solomon had planted on the roof along the abandoned clothesline.

The damp soil was starting to look loose and brown and somewhat smooth. Her shoes sank deliciously into it as she walked around picking up papers that had blown in overnight. Suddenly she stopped and looked over her shoulder. Behind her was something she had seen only once before, at Coney Island, and then it got washed away by the waves—her own footprints! Footprints were not something you made in this hard-packed city that forgot your passing as soon as you were gone. She stared over her shoulder at them following her, marking her path.

"Oops, hey, wait up!" It was Leroy, who came bounding after her, destroying her footprints with his own.

"Stop right where you are, man," she yelled. He froze, looking confused. Sorry for sounding gruff and wanting some-

163

where deep inside to make it up to him for all her months of meanness, Opie turned around.

"Look, what I meant was, you destroying my footprints, you clod," she said. He looked down unbelievingly.

"Lemme get this. *I* am destroying *your* footprints. Okay, I'm destroying your footprints. I got bigger feet."

"Leroy, you know what? You and me walk 'round this city every day and we never once seen our own footprints." He looked at her and his face softened, then broke out into a wide smile.

"I like that 'bout you, Oops. You always thinking 'bout things some new way. Yeah. It's like they roll out the concrete and we can't never make our mark on it."

"Yeah. And here we treat the ground right, it gets all soft and says, 'C'mon, just walk all over me 'cause I love it. You belong here.' "

Suddenly she sat down, pulled off her shoes and socks, and stood up, digging her toes into the velvet dirt. He watched her amazed, then sat down and took off his own. Opie started whirling around him. Together, with the growl of the cement truck and the hammering and the roar of the traffic as music, they laughed and danced until there was a flurry of footprints in a big circle in the middle of the garden. Opie stomped on the ground, then Leroy jumped up and down and Opie yelled, "Wake up! You not dead anymore. Wake up ground 'n' grow!" They didn't even care that the workers were watching as if they were crazy. Leroy hooted and chanted a crazy earth-waking chant. It felt like the garden had had a birthday.

"So, Oops," he said, his arm brushing hers as they stopped and began gathering up papers and trash, side by side, in their bare feet, "what's next? I mean, we getting through with breaking our backs or what?" He asked it as if she knew. Why did he always think she knew things?

"Leroy, I'm reading fast as I can. Ain't never touched no

164

dirt before, any more'n you. Think we gotta keep turning it over deeper and sifting. Maybe get those Rototillers the nursery man say he rents. Conley told me she even got a place on Long Island to give us a load of topsoil and manure and some trees and bushes. Might even come today!"

"Manure?" he said. "You mean like—cow shit?"

"Well, I didn't special order what *kind* of shit, Leroy, but I hear it makes things grow good." She smiled at him.

"We sure do need someone who knows 'bout this stuff."

"I got someone in mind," she said. "Just gimme some time. I be working on him."

"You mean Mr. Leshko, right?"

"Uh-huh."

"Look, Opie, I wanna ask you something . . ."

He stopped and looked shyly over at her, probably wondering if she was going to slam him shut again. She fixed her eyes on him so as not to see Joelle sneaking up behind him and sent him something soft in her, straight from inside. He caught it. A moment later Joelle tickled him and put her arm through his, so Opie closed off the little place she had opened to him.

They were tight now anyway, Leroy and Joelle, according to Joelle. Opie sighed. It was typical of the way things happened in her life. But even as she thought it, she knew something had changed, moved over just a little. The WILDCAT! power was still working in her, pushing her out of her misery.

Suddenly Joelle pointed down toward Second Avenue with a look of horror on her face. "*That* wasn't there before!" she said with an open mouth.

Opie and Leroy whirled around. On the wall of the building with the star, about six feet high in red spray paint, was a coiled cobra striking a Jewish star. The snake had black swastikas for eyes. She and Leroy had been so busy waking up the ground that they hadn't even noticed.

Anger flared up along an old pathway inside Opie, hardening her hands into fists, but there was no one to hit. Who do you hit when things happen? she wondered. You gonna chain the whole city to cement and sink it in the East River? The blame just seemed to spiral up and up like an old turkey buzzard over a carcass in Georgia. Her arms stiffened with not understanding it, closing her chest down tight. She wanted to cry as she walked over to beat her fists against the ugly thing.

Leaning her head on the wall, she breathed in all the way. The spray paint was so fresh you could still smell it. Then she remembered the place inside where she'd made things safe for times like this. The grass was soft there in the Sabbath Garden, just like the brown earth under her bare feet. She made herself take another deep breath to stretch out the tightness around her heart. Then she closed her eyes and noticed that someone had been busy planting flowers in her garden. She let go and lay back among them, expecting to fall on the hard cement of her life, but no, the soft petals were real. They held her up like a hammock and gave her back her power.

The sound of angry voices broke into her garden. She opened her eyes slowly. A clutch of old bearded men in black hats and coats stood on the sidewalk staring at the snake with swastikas, jabbering in that other language Solomon spoke. Some gestured angrily; some held their heads and bobbed; some lifted their arms to their Friend upstairs; some made fists; but all of their eyes pinned her to the wall like darts.

She turned toward them, her feet connecting with something coming up through the dirt. They fell silent and folded their hands expectantly in front of them, waiting maybe to see if she would make the monstrous thing go away. She dug her toes nervously in the dirt, feeling a piece of concrete they'd missed, embarrassed by having to face them without her shoes, these odd men in suit coats on this scorching day. Her mind stayed still and strong, even while her heart pounded.

166

"I'm very sorry," she said loudly, pointing to the wall. "Some stupid person did it last night. I want you to know, we been starting a community garden in this here lot. Gonna be beautiful—trees and flowers. We won't let nothing like this happen again, I promise."

A short man with glasses, somewhat younger than the others, spoke in an accent just like Solomon's. "Did anyone ask us if we wanted a garden by our shul? You could ask."

"You're right, sir, we should have asked," she said, aware that Leroy and Joelle were hiding behind her. "We been so busy getting started, we just plain forgot. Can we ask you now?"

"No—is the answer," the short man said. "If necessary, we can go to the city council and get an injunction to stop all this. Morris here knows our representative." Opie suddenly felt a bolt of fear as she understood that the impossible was really possible—they were dead set against the garden.

"You'd rather have garbage and weeds?" she asked them amazed.

"We would rather have a ton of garbage than *that!*" All eyes turned in unison to the coiled snake, then back accusingly to her, as if they had just caught her in the act of something disgraceful.

"Bring so much attention to this corner," said another man, shaking his finger at her, "and next thing they smash our windows, then they burn. We seen it happen, believe me."

Where was Solomon this morning? He went out every morning, and now when she needed him, where was he? Probably packing, the jerk. She sighed, feeling that this garden was some crazy dark tunnel leading nowhere and she was caught halfway there, not knowing whether to go forward or back.

"I got an idea," she told them, trying to sound bright and energetic as the workmen unrolled chain-link fencing along the sidewalk between the men and herself. "What if we paint over the thing and put a sign up there?"

"No, no, don't you see? Advertising is no good. Not on the shul. No good," said Mr. Glasses, shaking his head.

A tall, sunken-cheeked man with watery blue eyes and a long scraggly white beard, probably the oldest one there, elbowed him out of the way and stood forward, leaning on a cane. The others seemed to fall back as if he was their leader.

"So what would you put on that wall, young lady?" he asked in a loud voice that didn't go with his caved-in body.

Opie bit her lip and took a breath. She threw out her hand. "How about 'The Sabbath Garden, A Community Project'? You know, like a place apart from all that out there. Like the Sabbath." There was a murmur among them.

"What do you understand of the Sabbath?" asked the oldest man, squinting at her.

"That you set time apart to be quiet. Like you freeze and God says talk to me today, I'm lonely, right?" The workmen banged on the fence between them. "Sometimes we got need of *places* like that, too, 'specially in this neighborhood."

"And we'd like to invite you to come sit here, in the garden. There'll be a patio with chairs right over there," came Arianna's strong voice from her right elbow. "Why not get your grandson and the rest of the yeshiva boys, Mr. Kopinsky, and tell them to come up and help us. We could use help." More murmuring.

"We cannot allow it," said Mr. Kopinsky, pushing up his glasses. "It will be bad for the shul, and problems we got enough of already. We want you should stop." He pointed to the snake. "And you will get rid of that *thing*—today!" Much nodding.

"We have a board meeting tomorrow night," declared the watery-eyed man. "Let us talk of these things then." Some of the men seemed to agree, but others gathered around

168

Mr. Kopinsky, shaking their heads and arguing very fast and loud as if this was the biggest thing that had ever happened to them. As the men walked back into the building, Arianna put a hand on Opie's shoulder, and Leroy and Joelle gathered around, looking worried. Two new people had wandered over and Opie recognized them from the Sunday meeting.

"We *can't* stop," Opie said, as sure of that as anything.

"I'd better talk to you-know-who," said Arianna. "He'll work on them. Don't worry." She looked up at the snake.

"I'll get rid of this, Oops," Leroy said cheerfully. "They've got ladders and paint in the recreation center. Gimme an hour, you won't even know it was here. Man, you were great with those old fossils. They're just party poopers. No way they can stop us."

"Well, we don't want to find out if they can. I'm going to talk to Uncle Sol." Arianna ran off behind Leroy.

"Well, you gonna take a nap?" Opie asked Joelle, who was just standing there. She motioned to the newcomers. "Show these people where we keep all the shovels an' stuff."

Armed with rakes, wheelbarrows, and Leroy's sifter, they dug deeper into the soil that morning, turning it over and over, as the fence went up quickly all around them. Four more people came down and it felt like a big crew for the first time. The truck with the topsoil and manure arrived and dumped its smelly load over in one corner, not too close to Banjo's house. The nursery man set out five little bagged trees, which he said were apple and pear, and some shrubs, and told them to be sure and fill the holes with water and by the way, good luck. Opie signed for the delivery.

Leroy had placed the ladder under the snake and was covering it from the bottom up with white paint, but the thing bled right through. It took him most of the day, three coats of paint, and some swearing to really get rid of the ugly thing.

169

The double gate went in. The fence made the place feel safe, but Opie knew it could never lock out the people who hated or the city council.

Arianna arrived and was the first one to come through the squeaky new entrance. Solomon, in his black suit coat and hat, was second. They all cheered. He looked around open-mouthed, as if he was in some strange fairyland, although it really was just a sea of brown dirt.

"*Oy,* in such a few short days, a miracle!" he said amazed. Holding on to his cane, he bent down with a groan, dug his stubby hand in the loose dirt, felt its grain, smelled it, threw aside a cigarette butt and a sliver of brick. Opie held her breath as she watched him.

"You got a plan?" he asked them as they gathered around. "Make a good map before you plant. One bed here, one bed there, tomatoes over there, maybe a path to walk. And water. Where is the water, eh? I see in the catalog they got these hoses with holes along them to water a big space."

"Mr. Leshko."

"What is it, Opal?"

"You show us how to make this plan? Otherwise us bozos just gonna sit around and sift dirt all summer. Leroy here can't even water a houseplant!" The others laughed as Leroy nodded and they gathered in closer with a chorus of "yeahs" and "pleases." It was the first time they could see Mr. Leshko had something to give them. Leroy's eyes touched hers and she knew that he was hoping right alongside of her. But Solomon left them hanging.

"Much time I don't got these days, with packing and all. Also, Annike tells me of this little problem next door, eh? Let old Sol work on those knockers and see what comes." He patted Opie's shoulder. "You done a good job, Wildcat, the Most High bless you."

Then he walked out and around the new fence toward Second Avenue. Opie leaned on her shovel and followed his slow rolling progress toward the place with the star. He stopped to wave at her before he went in.

"Shit," she said.

"Give the man time," Leroy advised, touching her arm lightly. She smiled at him.

TWENTY-TWO

❦

Making Magic

IT WAS JUST AFTER SUNDOWN when Solomon swung open the heavy door of the place with the star on Second Avenue. He touched a little metal box on the doorjamb, kissed his fingers, and mumbled a short prayer.

"Come, come," he urged Opie, who hung back as Arianna walked through. Sabbath with Solomon in his apartment was one thing. But this was the strange place she had spied on in the fifth grade; the place where she had been told that children were sacrificed and curses put on people; the place of weird rituals, bobbings, mutterings, and names on the wall. Even though she knew it was Solomon's place, it still felt dark and dangerous and far out beyond the edge of anything she had ever known.

"I'm scared of all this," she said to him, half hoping he'd say, Okay, go on home, he'd handle this board meeting of the angry old men by himself. But no, he'd told them proudly that afternoon how sure he was that "his girls' " being there would make the difference in the vote about the garden.

And so here she was, dressed in her white summer Sunday dress and flats, tiny little earrings and pin, knowing the men's eyes were going to make holes all over her. The three of them walked up a plain, dimly lit hallway that looked pretty ordinary, with shiny wood floors and no pictures on the wall.

"Not to worry." Solomon patted her arm. Arianna walked

briskly ahead of them, her flowered skirt swishing, and to-night she had on a bra. As they passed a big basket on a table, she took a beanie, put it on, and offered one to Opie, who shook her head and wanted to say, Won't those old men be upset with you for wearing that? Why get them all prickly before we start with this mess? But Arianna wasn't much for paying attention to what other people were thinking of her. She pretty much did whatever she wanted—never mind what came.

They stopped for a minute at the open door of a large room with floor-to-ceiling books on shelves and long wooden tables with green glass lamps. A few men sat bent over thick, heavy books. Their lips moved as they labored down the pages, line by line, and there was a low murmur in the room, as though they hadn't learned to read to themselves yet.

"This is the house of study," Solomon whispered in her ear. "Here we learn and pray about the holy books—Torah and Talmud. Used to be when I was your age, we would come to the shul every night after sewing pants all day. Our stomachs were empty, but our minds and hearts, ah, they were always full."

They walked on down the endless hall and came to another open door leading into a much smaller room.

Around a table in the middle sat the old men who had yelled at her on the street yesterday. Solomon pushed her through the door in front of him and greeted everyone in a jolly voice. The men stared with solemn surprise; several of them whispered behind their hands. Opie noticed Mr. Kopinsky sitting back in his chair with a scowl. At the head of the table, the oldest man with sunken cheeks sat straight, his pale face perfectly calm.

"Rabbi Heschel," Solomon said, "here on this hand I would introduce my good friend, Opal Tyler, and I think my grand-niece, Arianna Litvak, you have met, no?"

"Yes, yes, Reb Leshko, we are glad to see such energetic

young ladies. Take a seat. Take a seat here by me." He patted
the empty chair next to him, his eyes on Opie. She and
Arianna sat down, one on either side of him. Opie fixed her
eyes on her hands, which were twisting in her lap. Every muscle was coiled up tight. Arianna was oversmiling nervously at
everyone around the table as Solomon took what must have
been his usual place halfway down.

"So tonight, *balebatim,* we will try to address each other in
English," said the rabbi. "Since we have such visitors, the last
order of business is moved up to first. Let us open with a discussion of the new—garden"—the rabbi leaned toward Opie
with a little smile—"the Sabbath Garden, this young lady tells
me." He rose, and all the others rose after him. Opie stood
last. Swaying slightly, he prayed in their special God language
and the others answered, "Amen," just like in the A.M.E.
Church.

"We will begin," said the rabbi, bowing his head toward
the others as they sat down. Mr. Kopinsky cleared his
throat. "Reb Kopinsky, I see you have something important to
say."

Mr. Kopinsky pushed up his thick glasses and rose as if giving a speech. His finger punched out the words like a politi-
cian's. "I want to say, do *not* forget Beth Israel over on Sixth
Street, how the people suffered just last year with the windows broken. Things are quiet here now. But if we have big
doings next door, it will happen to *us.* Yesterday already we
seen what will happen right on our own wall. The hate you
cannot paint over. Let us vote for our own safety." He sat
down to murmurs of approval.

"Reb Titlebaum." Another old frail man rose and looked
around with worried, fearful eyes.

"When first I came here to shul in 1930, it was a good clean
neighborhood. We were among our own people. Tonight I fear
for my life to walk here two blocks from Avenue A, so I must

174

take a cab. A cab! Two blocks! We are prisoners of these others who don't care about nothing, except hating and killing. I could weep for us. We are an island, all alone. We are dying. But a little while yet, we got to take care of our own." He sat down sniffing, shaking his head back and forth. Several around the table dabbed at their eyes.

"Ah, Reb Leshko. What have you to say to all this?"

Solomon stood up. Opie held her breath. "Morris is right," he began in his thunder of God voice. "We are dying, right here where we once belonged. Now I ask you, when a man separates himself from others, when he thinks, *They* are not like me, *they* are bad and *I* am good, what happens? Eh? The others feel pushed away, right? The man walks off and the others want to throw stones at his back, or his window, as the case may be.

"With the shul, it is like that. We been busy making ourselves an island in this neighborhood for years now. Everything that goes on around us, we been shutting it out. No wonder the people here think us strange, call us names even. Well, I, for one, have learned a lesson by living here among all those 'others.' And that lesson is this—we are all the same. It don't matter who. We want the same things. Opal here has been a good teacher to me on this account. She says that if you keep thinking about 'them' out there being against you, things start to happen that way.

"So, what am I saying?" Solomon leaned forward on the table and his eyes swept his audience. "I say that we stop turning our backs on this community *tonight,* right in this room, and start being part of things again. Here is a group of young people who have a dream to build something beautiful and good in the middle of all these ugly problems we got. I say give our blessing and *mazel tov* on this Sabbath Garden!"

There was an uproar after Solomon sat down, heads turning,

175

beards and fingers wagging. The rabbi struggled to be heard over the din.

"Let us take time to talk and then we will vote," he said and stood up, signaling Opie to follow him. In his little office, he closed the door and stood behind his big desk, bony fingers closed on top of his cane, long thin beard falling into two curled forks at the bottom. He looks like a wizard, Opie thought, all he needs is a tall pointy hat with stars.

"Such a noise," he said, smiling, and held out his hand. "Sit down." He sat, bones creaking as if it was hard to bend, and pulled his chair up close to the desk. "Now, young lady, I want you should tell me, *why* are you planting this garden?"

"Mr. Rabbi, sir, 'cause I thought maybe it would keep Mr. Leshko from moving away." Opie felt close to tears and held tight to the edge of his desk, hoping it would keep her from floating away. "Man likes gardens so much, you know, told me once he always wanna be a farmer, so I figured out a way to give him his chance."

The rabbi sighed deeply. His pale eyes looked far away. "Yes, what a terrible sadness to lose Sol Leshko, the Most High forbid it comes to pass," he said. "Sol is our brother. He is the heart of the shul. To lose him is like cutting off an arm." He leaned forward. "So you think he might stay? Has he said so?"

"No. He's still packing. But I got my foot in his door. We need him here. He's part of what makes this place great. You all are—I guess."

The rabbi stroked his straggly beard and stared down at the blotter on his desk, a quizzical smile playing at the corner of his mouth. He looked more and more like a magic wizard.

"You are friends with Sol?"

"Guess you'd say we learned to be friends."

He nodded gravely. "I see."

"Just wanna say one more thing, Mr. Rabbi. That garden,

it's for Mr. Leshko, like I told you, but it's for all the rest of us, too. I mean, us kids in this neighborhood never knew we could do something big like this before. Gives us kinda dignity, you know?"

"Hmmm. Well, how important it is to have dignity—that I know! Sometimes it seems there's less and less to go around these days." He rose. "We must go back."

As the rabbi walked into the room, the heated discussions died down to a few coughs and whispers. He stood at the head of the table and raised one arm. "If there is no further discussion, and I know there has been much discussion today—so I hope you have all had a chance to say your say—I call a vote. Those who wish to vote for letting the garden go forward will now raise hands." About half of the hands went up. One man stood up, counted, sat down, and wrote the number on a pad of paper.

"And now those against."

When the votes were counted, the paper man rose to say there were five for and five against. All heads turned toward the rabbi. He folded his hands and swayed with his head thrown back as if listening for guidance from above on this dilemma. No one breathed or moved. Opie had the feeling his vote carried a lot of weight.

"My vote—yes, my vote goes for the garden, *but*—only if it is properly supervised," the rabbi finally said. "Someone from our shul must oversee this undertaking from start to finish." Opie's heart did a somersault. "Is there one among us who will take on this worthwhile project?" She didn't dare to look at Solomon, but she did glance at the rabbi and thought she saw him wink at her. Man had some kinda wisdom, even if he looked like he could keel over dead at any minute.

The men looked from one to the other, shaking their heads, and Mr. Kopinsky broke out in a big smile. It was his smile that sent Solomon to his feet.

"Ah, Reb Leshko! May the Most High bless every seed you put in the ground and make it grow a hundredfold and more," the rabbi said.

Solomon looked very confused for a minute, then he threw up his hands. "Why not? Like you say, it is a most worthwhile project. If old Sol can make things grow out of pots, why not from the good earth, eh? And to have so many fine friends to share the work—a man is blessed."

"Then you will not be leaving us, Reb Leshko?"

"Well . . ."

"A garden does not grow in a week. Especially not a Sabbath Garden." The rabbi bowed his head in Opie's direction.

"I will settle with the landlord and unpack tomorrow!"

"*Mazel tov,* Reb Leshko! Welcome back where you belong." The rabbi threw out both arms and Solomon came up to hug him. Opie noticed a tear rolled down the rosy fat cheek and the sunken one alike.

There was a ruckus of *"Mazel tovs"* as eight hands reached out to shake Solomon's hand and pound his back. The rabbi pumped Arianna's arm, then Opie's, and turned to Mr. Kopinsky, who alone still sat quietly at the table.

"Reb Kopinsky, come. Congratulate the young ladies. I know you wish them well, my friend."

He stood up reluctantly, mumbled *"Mazel tov,"* and stretched out a hand to Arianna. Glancing at the rabbi as if the old man had asked him to jump off a bridge, he quickly shook Opie's hand. She knew it was probably the first time he had ever touched a black person.

"*Balebatim.* Back to work, back to work," cried the rabbi as Opie and Arianna thanked everyone and went out the door. Solomon waved, beaming them a broad smile as they left.

❧

TWENTY-THREE

The Fire
Within

"Do you believe it?" Arianna asked as they pushed open the door and went out into the cool night. "I mean, what did you say to Rabbi Heschel when he took you in there?"

"Oh, we just made some magic together," Opie said, shrugging mysteriously.

"Well, whatever it was, Uncle Sol was ecstatic. You could see that. He was just looking for a way to stay, I think. Opie Tyler, you did it! You made him stay! You're super amazing. You said you would and you did." They hugged each other tight. Opie let herself believe that she *had* done it. Her steps felt light and full of hope for the Sabbath Garden summer and for her life.

"Hey, let's go stand in the garden," Arianna said excitedly, turning south toward the corner. "We've never been there at night before." As they walked along the chain-link fence, only the edges of the garden were lit by the green glare of the streetlights. But in the dark they both suddenly saw that the ground near the entrance at the other end was strewn and heaped with garbage and paper.

"Oh my God, someone's trashing it!" yelled Arianna. As they raced around the fence and their eyes adjusted to the dark, they saw three boys slinging bags of trash and dumping gasoline all over. Opie knew in her heart it was Frank, and Arianna knew it, too.

179

"I'll get him! I'll get that dirty low-down bastard this time!" she screamed through clenched teeth.

"Be careful," was all Opie had time to say. Arianna ran fearlessly up to Frank, who was lighting the garbage with a wood torch.

"How dare you!" she yelled, trying to tear the flaming stick out of his hand. They struggled as the fire swayed back and forth above their heads for a few seconds, until Frank tossed the stick into the already roaring bonfire and stood waiting, inviting her next onslaught as if it were a game. The flickering orange light wavered against his face. He was smiling an empty smile and it made Opie's blood go cold. Arianna rushed ferociously at him, hitting, kicking, and cursing, but he stood tall, laughing, knowing before she did that he had clearly won this round.

Opie looked wildly around, paralyzed, torn between running for help or running to help. Everything ground into slow motion as the fire exploded with a whoosh. Frank grabbed Arianna's arms. She kicked and flailed savagely at him as he pulled her over, flung her against the back wall, and pressed his tall body against hers, covering her mouth with his, muffling her screams. As the flames roared up into a red inferno, the others fled, calling to Frank.

Banjo's house burst into a ball of fire. The old man cowered in the doorway, moaning and covering his head in confusion. Opie ran screaming to yank him away. He fell flat on the ground, scrabbling to crawl away from her as if she, and not the fire, were about to kill him. She jumped on top of him and beat wildly at his singed, smoking hair as he coughed and struggled. Grabbing him roughly by the waist, she pulled him up and out the gate, and sat him down against a building, yelling at him to stay.

The fire towered, twisting, crackling, and sparking into the night as she ran back through the gate. Somewhere in the distance, she heard a siren. Help was coming, and she had to keep her brother here until it did. *Had* to—somehow! As she raced toward them, she saw Frank's fist flash against Arianna's face; saw her slump in his arms. He had pushed his other hand up under her long skirt by the time Opie leaped on his back, knocking him forward full force into the wall.

This time there was not even a sliver of cool mercy stopping her rage. This time her anger burned hotter than the fire. As they rolled around close to the scorching flames, Opie locked her body like steel around his arms so that he couldn't hit her or get his knife or run away. He twisted and thrashed to break free like a fish in a bucket. She squeezed until her muscles shuddered with the strain.

Wheeooo-wheeooo wailed the sirens from all directions, still far away but closing the net. Frank's body stiffened. For one split second his eyes touched hers, wild, an animal caught in the jaws of a trap. And that trap was her power and his fear!

He bellowed, swinging her around, slithering partly out of her grasp and lunging for the gate. She hung desperately onto his leg, crying out at the stinging burn of being dragged over hot embers, glass, and garbage. But she would have held on right down the sidewalk until all her skin was scraped off if the police had not rushed through the gate and bumped right into Frank.

She let go and lay there curled and crying, spitting garbage and soot out of her mouth, in her torn, scorched, filthy white Sunday dress. A policeman knelt beside her, lifting her up, brushing the dirt gently off her face.

"What's happening here, miss?" he asked ridiculously, while the other policeman handcuffed Frank's wrist behind his back and shoved him against the fence. Fire fighters rushed past, their hoses snaking in behind. Columns of hard crystal water crashed into the fire, which sputtered and died without protest.

181

She stood up, holding her scraped raw leg. "He's the one who set the fire, along with his friends," she yelled over the hissing noise. Pointing to Arianna, crumpled down by the wall, she said, "And he tried to rape her."

"Bitch asked for it," Frank said through clenched teeth. His face contorted in pain as the policeman gave his arm a savage twist.

"Since you got him, Officer," she added, "he also ripped off a friend of mine and tried to kill me. This boy is one mean dude. Please keep him."

The policeman followed at her elbow as she limped over to Arianna. "I'll have to ask you a few questions, ma'am," he said insistently.

The girl, who was sitting against the wall, had pulled her torn skirt way down over her legs and covered her head with her arms. Opie stroked her hair and put an arm tightly around her. Arianna melted into her shoulder, sobbing and shaking, while the red and blue lights flashed over and over them.

"It's okay now," Opie whispered. "They got Frank permanent this time. Gonna take him away."

Arianna's hot tears wet her shoulder. Opie began rocking, the way Ma'am rocked when she sang, swaying softly, quietly, in the middle of the mud and chaos. She even began humming the chorus of "Nearer My God to Thee," because it was the only thing that came into her head.

The policeman pulled out his pad.

"I need your name and address, please." Opie interrupted her song to give him the particulars, then went right on humming.

"You say we should book this boy on arson, assault, and attempted rape?" the man asked. Opie nodded, wishing he would go away and leave them crumpled together with their song.

"Miss, would you like us to call an ambulance?" he asked Arianna, putting a hand on her shoulder.

She suddenly sat up, pushed the hair off her face, and wiped her eyes. "Oh, no, *don't* do that! Oh my God! Uncle Sol will *die*. I need to let him know I'm okay. Well, if I am okay." She felt the bruise on her cheek, wiped blood off her swollen lip, and pulled up the shoulder strap of her bra.

"You won't have to go find Mr. Leshko," Opie said, pointing toward the gate and rolling her eyes. "Here comes the whole hullabaloo right now." They looked at each other and groaned. Might as well pack up and all move to Queens.

Solomon was ahead of the others, who were waddling around the fence like a pack of penguins. He came babbling up, stepping gingerly over embers and garbage as if they would bite him.

"*Oy,* what happened here? *Gevalt!* Are you hurt? *Gott in Himmel.* Tell me quick! Annike, what's the matter?" He was beside himself, wheezing and gasping for air. Neither Opie nor Arianna had any idea what to tell him, so they clung to each other in silence. The policeman, after ascertaining that the old man was a relative, spilled the beans. Then came the bobbing and hand-wringing. And then came more bobbing and hand-wringing as the whole group gathered around and the word passed from one ear to the next, getting magnified as it went.

Arianna was mortified at their shocked stares and started to hide and cry again on Opie's shoulder. Even she was bobbing a little, fidgeting her hands.

"Tell them to go away," she whispered. "Just leave me alone." Solomon tried to gather her up in his arms like a child, but she wouldn't fit.

True to form, Mr. Kopinsky piped up to announce that he'd told them so. "How could I know the truth of my words, Sol, a dark sorrow on us all. This poor child. But you see now the wisdom of what I say. We will reverse our vote and be done with this mess."

Opie felt Arianna bristle and stiffen at his words. She inched up along the wall, gathering strength to face them huddled around her. They fell back slightly. Go to it, Opie thought, zap them and save the garden.

Arianna threw out her chin. "I'm okay—" she said, her voice on the edge of tears, but getting louder. "Now you listen to me. The boy over there getting into the police car—*he* did this. But *he* isn't the neighborhood. He's just one angry kid. We're not going to give up and go home because of some little thing like this. Anything good you've got to fight for, over and over. And we need you right beside us. I want to see one blooming glorious garden in the fall. I want to come back here and have a huge garden party where we can all eat and dance and see you give the blessing, Rabbi Heschel."

The rabbi, who had huffed up last, said, "Blessing? Who needs a blessing?"

"We do, right here," Arianna said, stamping her foot.

Solomon pulled Arianna to him. "*Oy vay.* What, in the name of the Most High, will I *ever* say to your parents—tell me that?"

"Tell them I learned more about life in a few weeks here than in all my years in Queens."

"And you really will come back for our harvest party?" he asked.

"Would I miss it?"

"Then it's settled," Solomon said. "*Mazel tov* to the Sabbath Garden! *Mazel tov* to a great harvest! Rabbi! Give us the blessing!"

The men looked at one another, openmouthed, in the dark. The police and fire fighters stood around watching the strange congregation at the scene of the crime. The rabbi shrugged and raised his bony hand over the cinders and garbage. In a loud voice he chanted, *"Baruch Atah Adonai . . ."*

The blessing finished, he turned to the waiting group. "May this ground soon be on fire with green bountiful harvest," he said.

"Amen," they all chorused back, Solomon the loudest. Mystified, the fire fighters exchanged glances, their hoses still in their hands.

"This board meeting is adjourned," the rabbi said, walking away. "Enough excitement already for one night!"

TWENTY-FOUR

❧

Lost and Found

THE SUBWAY PLATFORM WAS NEARLY DESERTED as Opie and her mother waited for the uptown train. Opie stared down the black tunnel where a distant *plink, plink* of water echoed and one tiny red light glowed in the dark.

She remembered her brother's face at the hearing that morning. Frank had sat on the bench trying to look as if he could mow down the world, but he didn't quite pull it off. Up on a high platform, the judge had looked as though he'd eaten tacks for breakfast and needed to spit them out. Judge man had loomed up as he asked his questions, and Opie could feel the scared under Frank's stony mask. All the bravado, all the light that said, "I'm gonna beat this thing," was gone.

She thought of Frank sitting on the edge of his bed in some stifling gray cell, waiting to be transferred to another stifling gray cell and then to that place upstate with bars on the windows and hard-ass guys who didn't hesitate to throw you against the wall if you made the slightest move that said, "Man, I am still free."

And all because of the way things were and because of a white girl who sassed him so hard that he had to have power over her and didn't even care about the gray cell. Opie sighed. It was like she'd told Solomon—you keep wanting more from life down here, you got to rob, rape, and maybe even kill to get it.

Her mother pulled a twisted tissue out of her purse and snuffled back the river of tears she'd cried all during the hearing. Ma'am had looked straight in the face of the sorrow that had been building up in her this year and fallen into an awful fit of wailing. Opie finally had to elbow her hard when she saw the judge fixing to warn her mother about disorder in the courtroom. Opie sighed again. Maybe wailing was a notch or two above sleeping life away.

"That child bound for trouble from the first time ever he set his little foot to the floor," her mother said suddenly and surely.

"You right, Ma'am," Opie said, looking at the dirty white tiles on the wall across the track, a good number of which had fallen off. "But one thing I know. Nothing you do gonna get him to go along. He got to find his own way to be free."

"Lordy, they gonna ruin him for the rest of his born days in that place. Done seen on TV what horror happen up there," Ma'am said, starting to sob again like her heart would break into a thousand pieces.

Opie turned away, feeling angry and merciless. "Gonna beat the crap outa him, that's what," she said. "Make him so mad, he come back here and kill us all after." She kicked a flattened paper cup off into the track.

"Done loved y'all 'til I ain't got no sense left. Can't do nothin' right." Ma'am blubbered so loud that the transit policeman was walking their way to investigate.

Opie leaned casually on the other side of the metal post as if she didn't know the woman. "Shut up," she whispered through clenched teeth. The policeman walked on by, tapping his billy club and staring sharply back at Ma'am. Suddenly Opie didn't care about the policeman, or the echoey station that magnified every word they said. She took her mother's shaking hand.

"Quit your racket and listen. You done right by us, you hear? Ain't not one shred of blame on you." Ma'am fell deeper into sobbing, and Opie had to put her arms around her to hold her up. "You and me been hanging onto this pretty picture we got of Frank," she said, laying her cheek on top of her mother's frizzled head. "But now we gotta say, 'Fine, bless you boy, go do it, whatever it is.' That's all. Let go, you and me. Right, Ma'am?"

Ma'am looked up and her crying lessened. Opie could feel the breeze of the approaching train blowing stronger by the second out of the tunnel. Suddenly all the hard push inside her melted as she looked at her mother struggling to let go her burden. The roar and screech of the train grew louder.

"Don' mean I'm gonna stop grieving," Ma'am yelled obstinately as the train whooshed screeching past them.

The doors flung open and they stepped into an empty car covered with ugly graffiti where they sat, side by side, in silence until past Spring Street. Then Opie leaned to say in her mother's ear, "Know what? You gonna learn to read. And I'm gonna teach you. Watch out, 'cause I got that in my mind now, and whatever I get in my mind, I can do."

"You crazy, girl," her mother said, but she smiled just a little at one corner of her mouth.

As the train rattled north through the dark tunnel past a pearly string of stations, a feeling like pigeons fluttering up from their roost rose in Opie and that feeling said something big was going to happen. She unfolded the carefully clipped newspaper article about the garden that had appeared in the Sunday *Times* yesterday. Her eyes ran proudly over her own words, and Solomon's, and the big picture of the two of them weeding the tomatoes. She closed her eyes and smiled. The pigeons settled back down, but barely.

As she stood watching Ma'am pull bent envelopes out of their brass mailbox in the downstairs hallway, Opie heard the familiar *click-click* of high heels on the marble stairs. She instinctively moved back into the corner in order to let Conk pass on down and out of the building without having to tangle with her. But Conk stopped on the bottom stair and stood silently begging for news of Frank.

"They sent him upstate for sixteen months," Opie said softly, looking away. Conk still didn't move. "He'll be okay," she added, shrugging uncomfortably, thinking, No, the skunk didn't leave no word for you, girl, didn't leave nothing behind but iron-hard anger. Why didn't she move on off the middle of the stair? Opie began to wonder. Let them pass, let it all pass.

Finally Opie looked up square at Conk. She drew in her breath. The girl seemed haggard. A deep line creased the smooth skin between her heavy, perfect eyebrows. But Conk's pain seemed all flat. The whole scene was squished flat—that's what it looked like to Opie. In that moment her whole body and mind shivered with the sure knowing that she would never again long for Conk, or allow herself to be drawn into the orbit of Conk's self-centered world. She had once and for all spun off and into herself. But for a second that raw place in her chest started to tighten up again, ready to be wounded, ready to deflect.

"Your brother is a bastard!" Conk hissed at her suddenly. Her eyes looked scared under the black mascara. Opie didn't want to hear about Conk's disappointment, didn't want her mother to know what Conk and Frank had done. Conk's problem was the way she lived her life. Not that Opie felt angry toward Conk. She just felt removed to another place where that old world of tangled problems seemed ghostly and unreal.

"C'mon, Ma'am, time for your reading lesson," she said brightly, pushing her mother up the stairs past Conk, who made a noise of frustration like a train screeching and stamped her heel. They continued on up and dropped down at the kitchen table without a word. Seemed like a whole chapter of their lives had closed—just slammed shut with a thud like a book.

Time to open another book, Opie thought as she headed into the bedroom to rifle her little library and get one of her easy readers from years ago. She snuck up on Ma'am and slid the book slowly under her nose.

"Ain't nothing but easy words," she said, creasing the book open at the title page.

Ma'am shook her head and snorted.

"You know your letters and sounds," Opie said hopefully, pulling up a chair.

"Don' know nothing," Ma'am said. "Better not start knowing now." But she rested her pointer finger on the word of the title and frowned at it.

They sat bent over the little book about a boy who ran away from home just like it was the Bible itself. Stuttering and stumbling into the sounds jumping off the page, they pushed on, heads together. Opie could feel a new thing growing in her mother and shoving them close.

The phone rang. Opie held Ma'am down in her chair, just like she'd been held all those years to homework chairs, and went, feeling very grown up, to answer it.

"Is this Bunie Tyler?" asked a deep, scratchy man's voice that Opie did not recognize. The voice had a pleasant roll to it.

"No. Just a minute," she said, completely puzzled at what man would be calling her mother. Didn't sound at all like Fish Boy Harmon or Brother George. What other men did her mother know? Opie felt a little thrill that maybe Ma'am had secrets. As she took a breath to turn around and tell her mother, she suddenly had to know. "Who's calling please?"

she asked in her most super-polite voice, just as if she were Ma'am's secretary.

"Is—is this Opal May?" the strange voice asked.

She hesitated. Something between excitement and violation began coursing through her. Who was this intruder who knew her middle name? She thought of hanging up, but finally answered him simply, "Yes," and frowned at her mother, who had scraped back her chair and was looking sideways at her with alarm.

"Opal, my name is Ellis Lee. You don't know me, but I knew you and your mother a long time ago. I happened to see your picture in the *Times* on Sunday, and I just had to tell you how proud I am of you and what you've done with that garden." The words rushed breathlessly out as though he had rehearsed them and was very nervous.

Opie held the receiver away from her ear, so that he would not hear the banging of her heart, not feel her falling into the deafening whirlpool of unfinished things in her life. Ellis Lee? The name was like a ten-foot-high neon sign in her mind. Ellis Lee of her daylong daydreams, who now sounded so close he could be around the corner at a phone booth. Suddenly she wanted to hang up. What if he *was* right around the corner? Oh my God, she thought frantically, swallowing much too loud.

"H—hello? Are you there?" the receiver was asking. Ma'am was starting to get up and come rescue her. Her whole life was staring her down. What do you say to the man you've waited a lifetime to meet? How ya doin', Dad? How's life treating you? Hey, what do you think about those Mets—pretty dismal, huh? By the way, where the hell ya been so long?

Opie cleared her throat. "Uh, yeah, I'm still here."

"Tell me how you got involved in that project?" Ellis Lee asked, staying with the garden rather than range into the forbidden territory of fatherhood.

"Oh, it's a long story, that's for sure," she said. "Been a good summer though. Feel like I learned a lifetime of stuff."

"You must be in eighth grade now, am I right?" There was a smile in his gravelly voice.

"Going into high school this fall." She stopped herself from finishing the sentence with "Dad"—a word she had never in her life said out loud. The unsaid word echoed in her mind. Did he think he was safe in acting like an old family friend? Twelve years and he talks about gardens and school, Opie thought. Finally she asked, "Where you calling from anyway?"

"Would you believe—Dayton, Ohio?"

"Well, I have to admit, it's not on my list of places people are from."

Ellis Lee laughed. "I've lived here for years. Came out here after I finished night school in New York. I work for a big bad corporation now." And you've got a huge stucco house with a pretty green lawn, right? Opie wanted to ask, like in my dreams. And a dog and a kid and a basketball hoop in the driveway?

"How's your mother, Opal?" he asked tentatively.

Opie glanced over at Ma'am, who had urgent questions splattered all over her face. She looked like she desperately wanted to know who it was but please don't tell her, both at the same time.

"My mother's doing just fine. She's working uptown. Been learning how to read better so's she can get her a really good job." Opie smiled at her mother. "Grandma'am died last year though." There was a silence. Opie rotated a pencil in the little plaster hole by the telephone, digging in deeper and deeper. "Uh—you got kids?" she asked, sweeping the pile of plaster dust off the counter into the trash can.

"Yeah. Two boys—and a wife. My oldest is seven and the youngest is four." Silence again. "Listen. You know, I was sure you'd moved."

192

"Nope. We gonna stay here forever, looks like. Neighborhood ain't too bad once you get to know it. But me, I'm going to college someday—like you, I guess." Why was this so weird? Opie took a deep breath. "Look, Ma'am told me 'bout you. I don't hate you, 'case you're wondering. I get mad at you for not being here sometimes. But my mother, she's pretty steadfast in your corner."

Ellis Lee laughed nervously. "She's got no cause for that."

"Why you say that? Both of us got serious respect for what you done with yourself." Opie was just starting to get a lid on this new volcano that had erupted in her life. She felt reckless, as though there was nothing to lose, nothing lost ever again. She wanted to put out the question that had pricked her heart so long. "When you coming on out here and see me?"

But Ma'am was already at her elbow, looking about as terrified as if she'd seen a robber coming in the window. Opie shoved the phone at her and ran into the bedroom to save the memory of his voice in her heart and to write down every word of their conversation in the embroidered book while the tears rolled down.

TWENTY-FIVE

❧

Violets in
the Grass

SUNDAY IN THE GARDEN was Opie's favorite time. She had lots of favorite times there—like just after dawn, when the dew was heavy on the plants and the traffic was still. And early evening, when things were soft and blue before the street-light's glare. That was when she and Solomon walked, arm in arm, from one end to the other and back again on the winding brick paths. It was then he taught her to admire every new sprout and leaf and talk to the plants just like he talked to the cats. The excitement of what they had done together settled down into pure peace and she felt the new green of the garden inside her, as well as outside.

But on Sunday nothing was slow, deep, or quiet. On Sunday the garden was always abuzz with busy people tripping over one another, laughing, shouting back and forth.

Sunday was big-project day. More and more people came each week to help out. One week it was the yeshiva boys up on scaffolding, painting a mural on the wall of the synagogue. It announced to all who crossed Houston Street, with much twining of plants and flowers, that this was, indeed, the Sabbath Garden. Another week someone mysteriously left a stone lion and they rolled it on logs to an unplanted place in the middle. Uncle Huey Chin wanted grass, like in the parks up-town, so they planted grass around the statue, which now sat in the middle of a small, slightly overgrown green. Close by stood the barrel of fire, painted red and ready for next winter as Opie had promised. A local artist had come the previous Sunday to weld a statue from junk they all found around the neighborhood and now it sat overlooking the broccoli patch like a scarecrow.

City council members and newspaper reporters arrived off and on to observe and catalog this phenomenon that was growing on the corner of the Bowery and Houston. They shook their heads because they saw all the separate and jagged pieces of this lost neighborhood—Puerto Ricans, African-Americans, Chinese, Jews, Italians, kids, priests, even Conley—fitting together smoothly in this little place.

On this last Sunday in August, Opie, for the first time since the idea of the garden had jumped into her mind, had over-slept. The gate clanged shut behind her. She stood, a little frumpled, with a piece of a dream still in her mind. She set her feet on the broken brick road that wound past and around raised beds of carefully weeded vegetables and brightly blooming flowers. The tiny fruit trees poked up bravely green and the morning glory vines on the fence were beginning to throw some shade on the patio, where Banjo and his friends relaxed in broken chairs they had salvaged from the street.

The air was cooler than usual and the veil of yellow haze had lifted overnight to show an almost blue sky. Opie closed her eyes and breathed in the coming fall, along with the magic of the garden. You could always feel this difference inside the fence. The air was fresher, the sunshine a little brighter. This place lifted her up and made her smile no matter where she was.

This Sunday's project—building a toolshed (with a little side house for Banjo as caretaker)—was already under way, with the Fourth Street Social Club in charge of sawing and banging. Solomon, pink-cheeked and happy, was bustling from one bed to the next, pointing with his cane and supervising.

Opie, for once unsure of where to go first, what needed her attention, knelt down to pull a stray weed poking up in the red petunias that lined the path. The garden was thriving; there were dozens of people weeding and watering and building and pruning, and each one seemed to move with purpose, as if he or she knew just what to do. Opie felt a sudden anxious pang of ownership as she knelt there. But sometime in the last few weeks the Sabbath Garden had grown beyond her, beyond Solomon, beyond them all. She sighed.

"You're late. We been slaving since seven, well—not quite—You better have a good excuse." A large hand landed on her shoulder. It was Leroy, on her case again, with a broad smile on his face. They had gotten to be comfortable friends and he didn't seem to hang around much with Joelle anymore. Opie had to admit she was always a little happier when Leroy was in the garden, too. She sat back on her heels. He sat beside her.

"Tired?"

"No, not exactly," she told him. "Just watching, sort of stepping back for once, you know, 'stead of jumping right in."

"Garden's grown up, huh?"

"Well, yeah, kinda has a life of its own."

"Pretty amazing how all this came into our lives and changed everything." He dug a finger in the soil under the petunias and didn't look up. "Listen. I finished the broccoli and tomatoes and cut the grass already. Ain't a whole lot left to do won't get done by someone. Why not you and me bike up to Central Park for the day? You could ride my brother's bike."

Opie's heart did a little fish flop; then she turned quickly away to concentrate on Solomon pulling the watering hose through the tomatoes. Sounded like Leroy Patterson was asking her on a date. She closed her eyes. Why had his words

196

taken her breath away? No one had ever asked her on a serious date. Before the summer she'd stopped believing that anyone ever would. Now she never had time to think about it at all. But if she had, she realized in that moment, to her surprise, it would have been Leroy she imagined asking.

But the boy could give some warning. I mean, here she was in cutoffs, no makeup, her most unfavorite earrings, and even no time to worry over the pimple on her cheek. She bit her lip. Now that she was through pushing him away, they did enjoy working together in the garden. But she worried that outside the garden maybe their relationship wouldn't exist.

"Well—you know, we really should—" This was ridiculous beyond belief. She threw down the weed in her hand. "Okay."

"Okay? You mean it? You really mean it, Oops?" There he was being goofy again, but she didn't care. The glorious day began to stretch out before her, open and exciting.

She poked him. "C'mon, let's go before someone tries to pull a guilt trip on us." They tiptoed down the path to the gate, looked back to make sure everyone was busy, opened the latch, pulled the gate quietly shut behind them, and burst into waves of laughter as they ran up the Bowery to Second Street.

The sun-dappled leaves of Central Park slid by and soft air brushed Opie's skin as they rode toward the boat pond. Her leg muscles were pleasantly tired after the long journey uptown through honking traffic. She smiled at Leroy's broad back ahead of her and pumped harder to catch up. They glided together off the road onto one of the paths and coasted down to the shallow, round pond where ducks floated along with dozens of brightly colored sailboats. Children ran and skipped and pointed happily as the boats dipped and swerved. A light breeze rippled the water into diamonds.

A little sound of celebration rose in Opie's throat as she sat down beside Leroy on a shaded bench to watch. It was all so

197

clear and sparkling, as though she was in another place just like the garden, only more. His hand rested between them on the weathered slats of the bench, the long fingers bent slightly, and in her excitement she had to keep herself from reaching down to touch them. One question kept flashing through her mind like a neon sign: Why had she been so ugly to Leroy? He, of everyone, had stayed by her, even when she could have scratched and bitten him bloody. Her chest tightened with the desire to take back all the mean words.

He smiled as he pointed to a man putting a model of a square-rigger flying a pirate flag into the water. The smooth bulge of muscle below the red of his T-shirt sleeve made her suddenly want to feel the weight and warmth of his arm around her shoulder.

She slumped down and pulled at the threads of her cut-off jeans. Something needed saying here, but it felt stuck inside her, lodged in the place where she still kept the confusion that had been her life before now.

She cleared her throat. His eyes were fixed on the water and his jaw just in front of his ear was working back and forth nervously. He doesn't know what to say, she thought, amazed, and it made her want to say it all.

"Um, Leroy," she began. He turned, but didn't rescue her with any words. He does have pretty eyes, she thought, and he looks right at me. "Look. Ain't easy for me to say I'm sorry, but that's what I'm saying here, okay? I been mad at life and feeling like, 'What's the use?' for so long, just turned me mean."

"I know," he said simply. Why did he make her uncomfortable sometimes being so straight on with things?

"Whadaya mean—you know?"

"You don't know half what I know. I seen you slipping and sliding and getting so down, you weren't you anymore," he said. "Things just took over and pushed you in a corner. I

198

know what it feels like—like you're a caged animal or something, and you wanna get out bad but you forget how. I wanted to help, but wasn't nothing I could seem to do right."

"You did help. You helped me let out what was eating me up. Wasn't no one else I could do that with."

"You knew I'd stand by you, didn't you?"

He folded his hands in his lap and looked sideways at her with the question in his eyes. She liked the way his eyebrows always arched in a question. What was it Arianna had said about Leroy—that he always asked the right questions.

"How come you don't hate me?" she asked.

"Hate you? Hey, I knew you'd come through the crazies. Sometimes life got to fall apart to be put together right. You the strongest girl I know, Oops. Pretty, too."

She snorted. "Now I *know* you a mud-face liar."

"Okay. I confess. It's your right hook I like so much." He smiled and punched her arm. "C'mon. Let's ride up to the lake."

They glided past the merry-go-round with its tinkling hurdy-gurdy music, under the brick tunnel—shouting and whooping to hear their echo—through the dusty green woods, and around the rippling water to a place where a gathering of trees invited them to stop.

Leroy parked the bikes and sat down against a thick tree trunk. Opie lay on the mossy grass and looked up through the funnel of dancing leaves at the sky. The city had fallen away from her that golden afternoon. Even the distant hum of traffic was drowned out by the buzzing of a bee in the grass near her. She turned her head to follow its busy darting movements among the little blue-purple flowers sprinkled in the overgrown grass under the trees. Suddenly she sat up with a start.

"Leroy, what's this?" she asked, picking one of the flowers and handing it to him.

"It's a violet," he said.

"That's what I thought." She sighed and turned over, chin in hands, to stare at the tiny forest of flowers. They looked just like the ones on the violet china plates, just like the ones in Georgia that Grandma'am used to pick under the cottonwood trees.

"Make me kinda sad—violets do," Opie said softly.

"How come?"

"Oh, they remind me of my grandmother. She liked violets."

"You loved her a lot, didn't you?"

"Didn't know how much 'til she died."

"Miz Tyler was so strong, seem like there wasn't nothing she couldn't do. People always said she was more super than ten men."

"You know, I remember she had the strongest hands. Sometimes I'd even see this kind of light streaming from her hands when I was a kid. Everyone always said I was just like her."

He smiled. "You bet. Can't move you one inch you don't wanna go, but when you wanna go, no keeping you away. She ever try to convert you?"

"Every day of my life. I held out though. She kinda let up after a while." Opie had gathered a little bouquet of violets. She buried her nose in their softness and breathed in the sweetness. Reaching over, she stroked his cheek with the flowers. He closed his eyes.

"I haven't believed in God for years," he said slowly. "Don't tell my father. You can't live on the Lower East Side of New York and believe in God."

"I don' know. Woulda gone along with that a year ago, but now I'm not so sure."

"You seen the light?" She could tell by the way he asked that he wanted her in darkness.

"Not the way you think. 'Member when I—well, you know—tried to kill myself last winter?" She stopped, wondering if she should tell him about the golden mist or stop safely where she was. She had never told anyone, not even Ma'am or Solomon, about the mist. Leroy leaned over and pulled her toward him to let her know that she was safe, no matter what. She rested against his shoulder.

"Something happen when I went unconscious," she said, lacing her fingers into his. "Like I been floating up over the room watching Ma'am trying to bring me back and then come this bright mist all around me, so amazing bright, like white light. Leroy, I tell you, I felt *good,* safe like you know."

"You think that's what it's like after we die?" She could feel his hand tremble slightly in hers.

"I *know* it is." It gave her goose bumps to say it. She looked up at him.

"I think I believe more in people being deep down good, like God's inside them."

"Yeah!" Opie said excitedly, suddenly connecting up some loose ends. The words rushed out. "Solomon taught me this great thing about there being a garden inside you, and you cultivate it and plant it and water it and then you can go there anytime, no matter what crazy stuff's happening on the outside. Maybe that's where we meet God—inside us."

He was staring at her, his face very close to hers, and then his teeth flashed white as he smiled his broad smile. "I love talking to you. Always get the feeling I'm going someplace new."

He put down the violets, very gently, and twined the fingers of his other hand in hers. They sat for a long time, cross-legged, looking into each other. People walked by on the path, squirrels scolded loudly, but nothing could make them move a muscle.

Opie saw herself in Leroy's eyes and with each passing moment she felt more beautiful, more special, more really her. Instead of not believing it, she dared to believe it more deeply than she'd ever believed anything and it made her cry. It was as if a river of love had been dammed up in her chest and now she could let it rush out.

He leaned back into the grass and drew her to him as she shuddered and sobbed on his chest until the front of his T-shirt was completely soaked. His strong arm held her as she lay still, feeling clean and new, feeling the sigh of his breath, feeling him alive in every pore of her skin. Or was it herself she felt alive in every inch of her? She couldn't tell the difference.

His fingers ran through her hair over and over as she nuzzled into his neck and put her arms around him. She closed her eyes and felt his heart racing against her cheek.

"You and me are going somewhere—that's clear," he said after a while, pulling away and raising up on his elbow. "Question is, are we gonna go there together?" He began kissing and nibbling her fingers, making her giggle. "Say yes," he demanded, tickling her mercilessly. She writhed in helpless laughter, begging him to stop. "Say what?" he asked, continuing his attack. "Tell me yes."

She pushed him away hard, suddenly afraid of letting it all be, suddenly wanting to build a wall around herself because that was what she'd always done. Men left. They hurt you, made you dull and dead, like Ma'am. She had told herself sometime long, long ago that there wasn't no way this girl gonna take a chance on no stupid boy, all the while hoping it wasn't true.

"You can't push me away again, girl," he said, grabbing her wrists and pulling her face to within an inch of his. "I won't let you. I *love* you." He let go and they both stared in wide-eyed surprise.

"You do?" she asked stupidly, her wall crumbling.

"Only for about a year. You just stone blind."

Then Opie did something she had never done in her life. She kissed him on the mouth, soft and long, very long. And he kissed her back, as they lay on the mossy grass among the violets.

202

TWENTY-SIX

✤

The Garden
Party

OPIE PUSHED OPEN THE APARTMENT DOOR, stumbled through the hall, and fell into the kitchen chair, where she began to cry. It had been coming all morning, this overload, as she ran around setting up tables and chairs in the garden and lacing the fence with crepe paper streamers and balloons. Ma'am turned around from scrubbing the counter and stared at her.

"Now you gone and deep-fried yourself," she said. "I seen it coming—all this party, party, party. Go lie down."

"Lie down!" Opie could hear herself screaming. "The party's gonna start in an hour and I'm not even dressed and all you can say is, 'Lie down'?"

"Lord, you gonna fizzle your brain with all this. Stop 'fore green smoke start shooting out your ears." Opie had to smile at the idea, but she let Ma'am take her arm and lead her into the bedroom, now neat and newly painted peach, with the curtains of rich creamy lace that Solomon had given her. They had done a flurry of housekeeping in the last few weeks.

The Bible lay open on her mother's bed. Just last week she had started on the Gospel of Matthew, determined to piece her way through the New Testament. She'd lost a little weight, too, and had her hair done. The yellow pills sat on the vanity, but Opie no longer counted them to see how many her mother had taken. This week they'd shampooed the shag rug on their hands and knees and cleaned Frank's room, putting his stuff in boxes. Then they threw open the iron curtain and stood there smiling at each other.

Opie sat obediently on the bed and turned the clock to face her. Ten-forty. She'd been up since six. Ten-forty-one. Oh no. Don't pass, time, she thought. She took the embroidered book in her lap, then she closed her eyes and tried to breathe. It was useless. A thrill-dread shot up like a geyser through every cell in her body, exploding any sense of calm. She opened her eyes. Ma'am was using the carpet sweeper on the rug again. Born-again clean freak, thought Opie. Then as she reached out to touch the flying birds in the lace curtain, she knew who it was she most needed to see.

Almost without thinking she pulled new jeans and a red shirt out of the closet—red for Solomon. Only a little more than an hour. She showered, pulled on the clothes, and made a swipe across the steamed-up mirror. Her face was clear today, eyes like shining black diamonds. The hair, which had been chopped-off fuzz, had grown over the summer to a respectable soft halo around her face. And her face had changed—the mouth was sexier now that it knew how to kiss, the cheekbones higher, the color like rich earth in the garden. Leroy was right about her being pretty, she decided in that moment before the bathroom mirror. Even her breasts had filled out the double-A bra she'd been uselessly wearing for two years.

"Back before noon!" Opie yelled to her mother as she slammed the door. Four at a time, she ran down the marble stairs to the second floor and knocked on Solomon's door. Please be home, she begged. She glanced over her shoulder at the orange-and-black-striped "WILDCAT!" and smiled. Conley still hadn't convinced the landlord to paint the halls, but she kept trying. There was a rustling in Solomon's apartment and then the bulging blue eye in the peephole, just like that first night.

"Ah, Wildcat, come in, come in," he greeted her, throwing open the door and pulling her in as he spoke. "I'm only just now having breakfast. So much to do down there." He'd been in the garden all morning, too.

Opie slid into the chair at the table and watched him shuffle over from the kitchenette. He's lost weight this summer, she thought, and his step is surer, not so much like a spinning top about to fall over. His eyes were always brimming over with a merry excitement.

On the table was a plate with something weird that looked like a midget goblet. Standing up in the goblet was, of all things, an unshelled egg. Solomon sat down, took up a spoon, cracked the shell, and dug in like it was ice cream with hot fudge.

"I'd throw up if I had to eat breakfast with you," she said with conviction, wrinkling her nose as she looked away.

"*Oy,* praise God you live upstairs." He put down his spoon and wiped the dripping yellow egg out of his beard, grinning. "You can look again—I'm finished."

"You know," Opie said, leaning her chin in her hands and smiling back at him. "I always think how funny it is we get along so good—us being majorly different."

"Not so funny," he replied, "us being so 'majorly' same after all." He laughed and folded his hands over his belly, which looked round and white as an egg itself. "Ah. You look to light up the world, Opal. I think you got a sweetheart, eh? Am I right? Tell me true."

"You don't miss nothing, do you?"

"Aha!" Solomon burst out with a self-satisfied twinkle in his eye. "Well, a hard worker he is, that Patterson boy, and handsome, too. I had my eye on him all summer." The old

205

man leaned toward her. "See, you believe in yourself and what happens? All things come to you."

Opie sighed. "This harvest party gonna come in less than an hour."

"And you are not excited?"

Opie looked out the window at Second Street. The sidewalks were as dirty and cracked as ever. Winos crowded the stoops and an abandoned car across the street was slowly being stripped down to the bare bones. "Yes and no," she said slowly.

"No? Why no?"

"Seems kinda like an ending of something I wish could go on forever," Opie said. The subway rumbled, horns honked impatiently. Opie looked back into the room.

"Now let me see. You survived a robbery, a broken heart, a gunshot wound, and back-breaking work—and you want more?" Solomon chuckled and pulled on his beard as he looked at her. "I, for one, am ready for a little rest," he added.

"But it was so special, so magic. And now it'll be—well, you know—just the same old place, same old routine."

"Ah, but here's the question," he said, reaching out to take her hand in his. "Is it the same old you?"

Opie thought about that, closing her eyes and trying to remember back across the summer to a time that seemed veiled and far away.

"No," she answered. "Now I have hope . . . for everything."

"Well, of that I am 'majorly' glad," he replied, grinning at her as he walked over to put on his black suit coat in front of the mirror. "I think your hope has changed this place. I feel it on the streets. I see it in my neighbors' eyes."

"You really think so?"

"Of course. You think that garden is just a place with plants dying in the frost? It's a beautiful symbol of what is happening inside all of us." He spread his arms as if to encompass it all.

206

"Well, 'least it's an excuse to talk to each other and stop all this hating that tears us apart," Opie said, smiling at his drama.

"When people see they can make a little miracle together right where they live, I tell you they get dignity," he added, shaking his finger at her.

"Dignity or no, I still don' want it to be over."

"Over? Who said over? Ten years from now you'll come back and a new crew of kids will be weeding the tomatoes! You'll see. And listen, don't forget the garden we been planting in here," he said, tapping his heart. "That one never goes away."

Opie closed her eyes and took a long, slow, fragrant breath. "Come for a walk with me, Mr. Leshko. Can you see the morning glories and red petunias?" she asked him.

He was silent a while. "You planted them just for me, didn't you?"

"Mm-hmm."

"A man is honored," he said. She smiled at him as he tried to smooth his little tufts of hair that would never lie down. "Do I look good enough for the evening news, Wildcat?"

"You look totally rad, Mr. Leshko," Opie told him, sliding out of her seat and going to give him an over-the-shoulder hug.

Upstairs, Ma'am was pacing aimlessly here and there, rearranging magazines on the new coffee table and flicking at imaginary pieces of dust. Opie walked over and put her arms around her mother.

"I wish my father could be here for this," Opie said.

"When it's right, he be here," Ma'am replied, stepping away to look at her. Then she walked into the bedroom and came back carrying a package wrapped in bright paper that she shoved into Opie's hands.

207

"What's this? Ain't my birthday for another three months," Opie said.

"Just go on, will you?"

Opie pulled the paper off slowly. Inside was a little gold frame with a wide mat and two tiny, creased, square black-and-white pictures, the kind you get four for two dollars in the photo machines up at Grand Central Station. Opie stared closely at first one, then the other. A man sat grinning with a bright-eyed two-year-old girl in his lap. She was all dressed up in a frilly white dress with a bow on her little pigtail. In one of the pictures she pointed up at the camera. Opie's heart began to pound.

"They're not much, I know. But they're the only ones I ever had of you and him," Ma'am said apologetically. "Told me he had the hardest time making you sit still, you rascal."

Opie smiled and touched the pictures, unable to take her eyes off them. She had never imagined herself a baby. Until now her memory had started at the age of five with her school pictures.

"This is the best thing you could ever give me," Opie said. "Like you just gave me back something I lost."

Ma'am sat down and Pee Wee immediately jumped up in her lap. Ma'am tried, not very successfully, to look calm. Protesting all the way, she had finally agreed last week to the dreaded and not-so-little-anymore cat coming to live with them. Although Ma'am attempted to avoid her, Pee Wee refused to cooperate, mercilessly seeking her out wherever she was.

Opie walked back into the bedroom to put the picture on her nightstand. She walked out, then walked back for one more look before she went to answer a knock on the door. It was Leroy in his best clothes grinning down at her. Opie suddenly thought how much he looked like her father, broad-faced and kind with smiling eyes, and also determined, like her father was, to reach quietly for something beyond the ordinary.

So all this time, Leroy just the spitting image of my father, she said to herself. "My father," she repeated under her breath and the sound brought up a little squeal of delight.

"What's that you said, Oops?" he asked, leaning toward her to hear better.

"Oh, nothing. Let's go," she said. A shiver of happiness passed through her from head to foot at the thought of her life, which had led her from what had seemed like endless night to this bright fall afternoon.

"Hey, Oops!" Arianna called out as she came running up behind them on the Bowery, skirt flying as usual. Opie and Arianna smiled at each other for a long minute, then embraced, their two hearts pressed together, opened forever by all they had shared.

"God, did I miss you! Hi, Leroy!" Arianna said breathlessly. "There's just no way anyone back home can understand."

"I'm not surprised," Opie said, putting her arm around Arianna's waist as they walked. She thought how she would not have dreamed of doing that two months ago and how now it was an automatic, fluid movement.

Solomon and her mother were not far behind. They moved in a large, chattering group down toward the garden. Arianna piled question on top of question. Had they put Frank in jail and how were her green peppers doing and had the yeshiva boys finally showed up to work and . . . Suddenly she stopped and put her hands on her hips.

"Wait a minute. What's this?" she asked, pointing to the fact that Opie was holding hands with Leroy. Opie hadn't even noticed, it seemed so natural. Opie shrugged, but she knew her eyes were dancing as she looked up at Leroy. Just to shock Arianna and do something no one would have ever thought she'd do a month ago, she gave him a loud kiss on the cheek. He looked embarrassed, but pleased. Arianna's mouth dropped the proper amount, then she laughed and twirled around.

"I knew it! I knew it! Another notch in my matchmaker's belt," she chanted. "I *knew* you two were made for each other. Of course you were definitely a hard case, you jerk," she said to Opie, then gasped as they entered the garden, which was brimming with people—everyone from Banjo and his friends (who had gotten new suits at the mission for the occasion) to city council members, Rabbi Heschel and the clutch of bearded men from the synagogue, and all the people who had turned over a handful of soil along the way. It took Opie's breath away, too.

Balloons and streamers decorated the fence, a band was playing salsa music, members of the Fourth Street Social Club pounded on bongos while the Bowery men danced with their bottles in full view. Rosie, Conley, and others from the building had been cooking the harvest into a feast that was spread magnificently over the tables. Knishes enough to feed an army from Yonah Schimmel's across the street sat next to Marita Perez's fried green bananas. And in the middle of it all, the same artist who had created the junk scarecrow had piled and sculpted a monstrously large and colorful centerpiece of flowers and vegetables from the garden.

People milled on every inch of the winding walkways, bending to admire each perfect plant ripening in the warm full sun. Buddy Cevasco had stopped throwing paper airplanes out of the third-floor window to make an appearance, and over in the corner, arms folded in an imitation of indifference, was Conk. Even more amazing to Opie, over in another corner a band of Jewish men in black coats started to play a wild, tinny kind of music on the fiddle and accordion. There at the front,

210

swaying as he played the clarinet no less, was of all people, Mr. Kopinsky. There was an accident on Houston Street as people from the cars going by slowed and strained their necks to see what was going on.

"This is indeed a miracle!" Solomon said in her ear. He squeezed her arm. She let herself feel the joy of knowing that it was the power of her wanting and her imagination that had made it all happen. And if she had done this and now it seemed so easy, what else could she do next?

There were speeches and even awards, and multiple blessings by Rabbi Heschel and Father Basilkowski, ceremonial plantings and presentations of the harvest to various officials, then more music and singing and much clapping and cheering. The TV crew showed up just in time to film Solomon stopping everything to give a toast, proclaiming proudly in front of everyone that Opie was the driving force and vision behind the garden and that she had kept it going day after day when people, including him, didn't believe it possible. Then Opie stepped forward, eyes shining, to say that this neighborhood had found its soul here in this magic place and she was proud of everyone who worked on it.

She and Solomon smiled at each other from across the circle of people as if they were in the just-before-waking part of a good dream they wanted to remember forever. As the crowd began to thin and mill again, his eyes fixed hers. She walked over to him and shook his hand.

"Yes, sir, Mr. Leshko, we have done a big *mitzvah* here," she said, remembering the word. Something made her want to cry, so she did, and Solomon started to snuffle, too, as they began a walk around, just the way they had at twilight so many evenings that summer.

They didn't speak to each other; they just kept walking around and around, arm in arm, tears rolling down their cheeks. Opie knew the way by heart—up by the tomatoes, around the stone lion, out the broccoli path, past the lettuce and herbs, slowly by the flower garden, and back along the petunia path by the garden shed to the gate. People smiled and turned to watch them pass as if they were far away wandering in some secret, wonderful, and unreachable green place in the far corners of the heart.

GLOSSARY

Some of the characters in *The Sabbath Garden* occasionally use words in Yiddish, Hebrew, and Spanish. What follows is an alphabetical glossary for easy reference and pronunciation.

Yiddish is the expressive and wonderful language of the eastern European Jews, who flooded into the Lower East Side of New York from about 1880 to 1925. It is a combination of German, Polish, Russian, and Hebrew and is written in the Hebrew alphabet. Hebrew is the language used by Jews for prayer, and is now spoken in Israel.

balebatim *Hebrew* (bol-*bot*-em) community leaders, board members of a synagogue

bodega *Spanish* (bo-*day*-gah) small grocery store

brujo *Spanish (broo*-ho) male witch, sorcerer

bubeleh *Yiddish (bub*-eh-leh) darling, sweetie

caray *Spanish* (car-*ay)* damn

chutzpah *Yiddish (huts*-pah) someone with a lot of nerve, gutsy, arrogant

felix compleaños *Spanish* (fail-*eez* koom-play-*ah*-nyos) Happy Birthday

gevalt *Yiddish* (ge-*vahlt)* a cry of fear or astonishment

gonif *Hebrew (gone*-if) thief

kaddish *Aramaic (cod*-dish) the Jewish mourner's prayer

khazer *Yiddish (khahz*-zer) someone who takes advantage of you, who is selfish, dirty, a pretty awful character

kippah *Hebrew (kee*-pah) a round skullcap worn by Orthodox Jewish men at all times and by other Jews for worship and ceremony

mal Judío	*Spanish* (mahl hoo-*di*-o) bad Jew
mazel tov	*Hebrew (mots*-el tuv) congratulations, good luck
mishegoss	*Yiddish* (mish-eh-*goss)* craziness, nonsense
mitzvah	*Hebrew (mitz*-veh) a good work, a kind deed
nadadora buena	*Spanish* (nah-dah-*dor*-ah *bway*-nah) a good swimmer
schmooze	*Yiddish* (shmooze) gossip
Shabbes	*Hebrew (Shah*-biss) The Jewish Sabbath celebration, which begins at sundown on Friday and lasts until sundown on Saturday. Orthodox Jews do not do any work on Shabbes, not even turning on and off the lights.
shul	*Yiddish* (shull) Jewish synagogue, which was also a place of study, like a school
shvartzer	*Yiddish (shvart*-zer) black person
spic	derogatory term for an Hispanic-American
Talmud	*Hebrew (Tol*-mud) books full of commentaries on the Torah, studied and discussed daily at the shul
tchotchke	*Yiddish (tschotch*-keh) an unimportant little thing
Torah	*Hebrew (Toe*-rah) the five books of Moses from the Old Testament
yarmulke	*Hebrew (yah*-mul-keh) a round cap worn by observant Jews

ABOUT THE AUTHOR

PATRICIA BAIRD GREENE has been a newspaper reporter; an editor of *New Roots,* a national magazine on alternative energy and life styles; and a social worker on New York's Lower East Side, the setting of *The Sabbath Garden.*

About this novel, she says: "After I moved to the country, the voices of the city kept pestering me. My memories of the bright fabric of diverse people living up against one another and learning to work together to make a community out of that desolate place wove into a story that told itself."

Mrs. Greene, currently at work on her second young adult novel, lives in a cooperative community in Gill, Massachusetts, with her son. An artist and graphic designer, she also loves working in the garden and exploring nature.